VERSAILLES
MY FATHER'S PALACE

Maïté Labat
Jean-Baptiste Veber
Stéphane Lemardelé
& Alexis Vitrebert

Life Drawn

**Maïté Labat
Jean-Baptiste Veber
Writers**

Alexis Vitrebert
Artist

Stéphane Lemardelé
Layouts Artist

Original Concept by Maïté Labat

•

Benjamin Croze
Translator

•

Fabrice Sapolsky
US Edition Editor

Amanda Lucido
Assistant Editor

Vincent Henry
Original Edition Editor

Jerry Frissen
Senior Art Director

Fabrice Giger
Publisher

Rights and Licensing - licensing@humanoids.com
Press and Social Media - pr@humanoids.com

VERSAILLES: MY FATHER'S PALACE
This title is a publication of Humanoids, Inc. 8033 Sunset Blvd. #628, Los Angeles, CA 90046.
Copyright © 2020 Humanoids, Inc., Los Angeles (USA). All rights reserved. Humanoids and its logos are ® and © 2020 Humanoids, Inc.
Library of Congress Control Number: 2020900171

Life Drawn is an imprint of Humanoids, Inc.

PARIS. SUNDAY, MAY 19, 1935.

Jacquemart-André Museum

HELLO, CHRISTIAN.

HELLO, MR. HENRI.

YOU'RE NEVER GOING TO CALL ME BY MY LAST NAME, ARE YOU?

IF I MAY, THERE CAN ONLY BE ONE MR. DE NOLHAC, MR. HENRI.

I'LL TAKE THAT AS A COMPLIMENT.

HOW IS MY FATHER DOING TODAY?

HE'S BETTER, HIS NASTY COLD IS GONE, BUT HIS LEGS ARE CAUSING HIM A GREAT DEAL OF PAIN. AND HIS HEARING IS GETTING INCREASINGLY WORSE, I'M AFRAID...

THANK YOU, CHRISTIAN. I'LL GO UP AND SEE HIM.

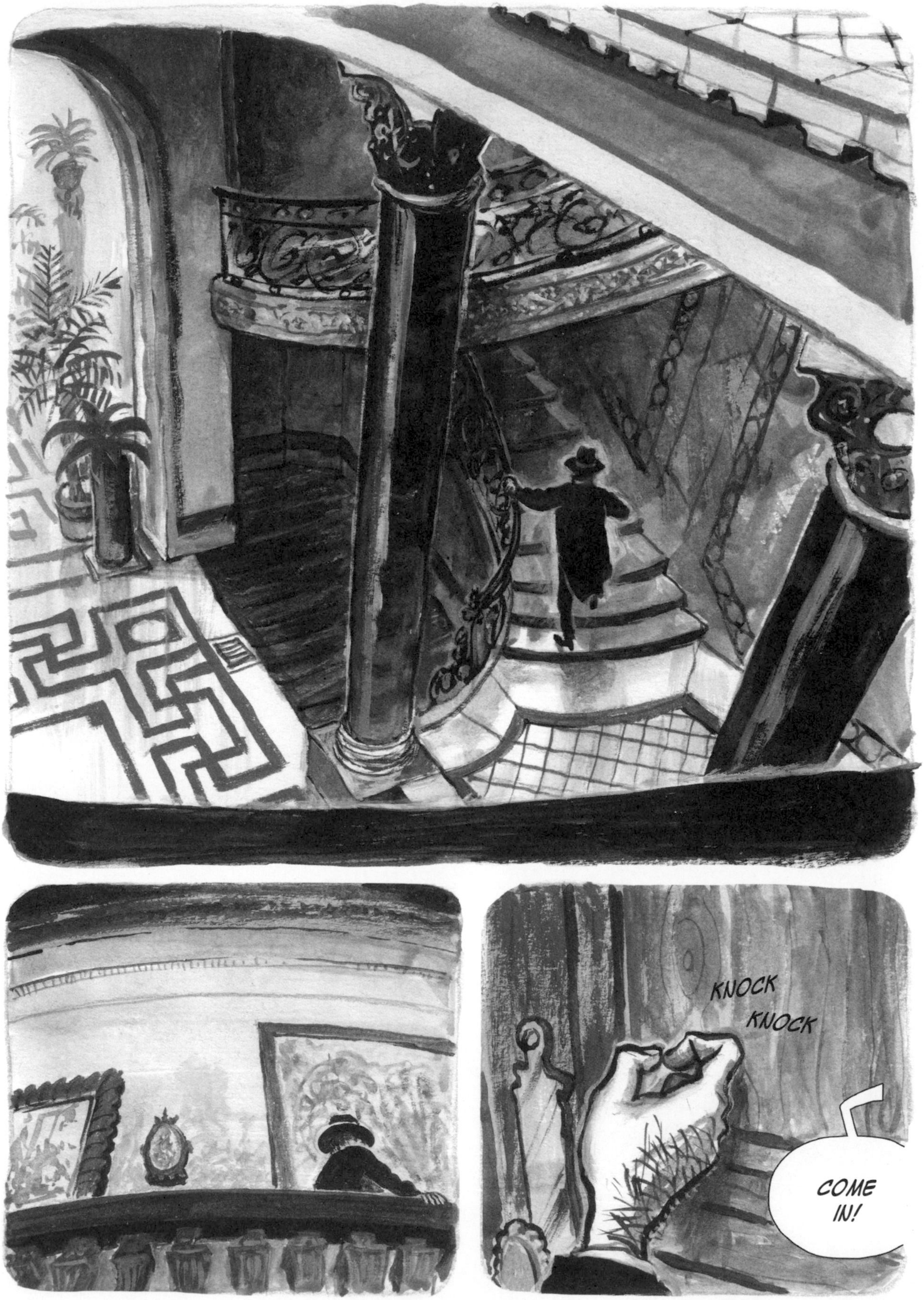
KNOCK
KNOCK
COME IN!

HELLO, FATHER.

AH! HENRI!

DID YOU RUN INTO ANDRÉ? HE JUST LEFT.

NO...

I'M TOLD YOUR HEALTH IS *IMPROVING* BUT YOUR LEGS ARE STILL SORE.

ONCE MORE, I SEE THAT MY SECRETARY IS UNABLE TO *HOLD* HIS *TONGUE.*

I KNOW WHAT YOU'RE GOING TO SAY, AND I *DON'T* WANT TO HEAR IT... I CAN *STILL* RUN THE MUSEUM FROM THIS OFFICE!

IF YOU THINK POLITICIANS RUN THE COUNTRY FROM THE *STREETS,* YOU'RE WRONG!

YOU HAVE *MORE* THAN EARNED THE RIGHT TO A LITTLE *IDLENESS--*

CERTAINLY NOT!

IT JUST SO *HAPPENS* I'M IN THE MIDDLE OF *WRITING.*

AH, AND WHAT IS IT THAT YOU'RE WORKING ON *NOW?*

VERSAILLES.

I'M WRITING DOWN MY MEMORIES BEFORE THEY DISAPPEAR WITH ME...

I SHOULD HAVE DONE SO A *LONG* TIME AGO.

FATHER...

FORGET ABOUT IT, HENRI.

SEND CHRISTIAN UP. HE TAKES NOTES WHILE I DICTATE. MY EYES NO LONGER ALLOW ME TO WRITE.

YOU'LL SEE FOR YOURSELF, I AM STILL PERFECTLY *CAPABLE* OF WORKING.

I NEVER KNEW WHERE MY FATHER GOT HIS ENERGY FROM, THE KIND HE HAD USED TO SERVE THE JACQUEMART-ANDRÉ MUSEUM AND, BEFORE THAT, ONE OF THE GREATEST PALACES IN THE ENTIRE WORLD...

6

Chapter 1
ARRIVAL IN VERSAILLES

OCTOBER 1887.

WE ARRIVED ONE MORNING, AFTER A LONG TRIP FROM PARIS. OUR HORSE-DRAWN CARRIAGE, WEIGHED DOWN BY ALL THE LUGGAGE, HAD HAD A HARD TIME MAKING IT OVER THE CÔTE DES GARDES.

ARE WE *THERE YET,* PAPA?

MY BROTHER AND I WERE EAGER TO EXPLORE OUR NEW PLAYGROUND, BUT I FELT A KIND OF TENSION GROWING IN MY FATHER.

HERE WE ARE.

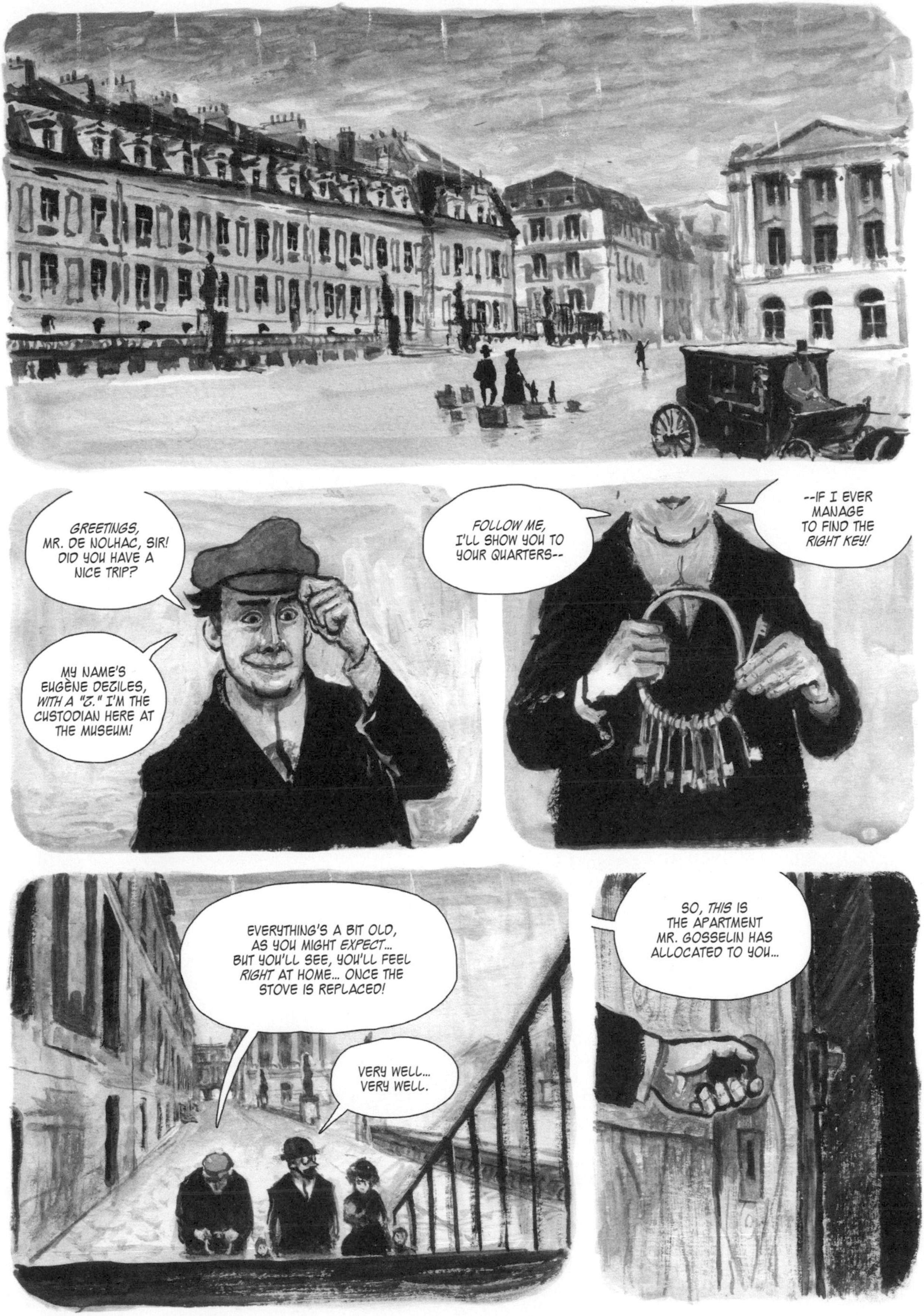
GREETINGS, MR. DE NOLHAC, SIR! DID YOU HAVE A NICE TRIP?
MY NAME'S EUGÈNE DEZILES, WITH A "Z." I'M THE CUSTODIAN HERE AT THE MUSEUM!
FOLLOW ME, I'LL SHOW YOU TO YOUR QUARTERS--
--IF I EVER MANAGE TO FIND THE RIGHT KEY!
EVERYTHING'S A BIT OLD, AS YOU MIGHT EXPECT... BUT YOU'LL SEE, YOU'LL FEEL RIGHT AT HOME... ONCE THE STOVE IS REPLACED!
VERY WELL... VERY WELL.
SO, THIS IS THE APARTMENT MR. GOSSELIN HAS ALLOCATED TO YOU...

I DON'T KNOW IF MY MOTHER EVER REALLY MANAGED TO APPRECIATE VERSAILLES. SHE TRIED HER BEST, THOUGH.

I'LL LET YOU GET SETTLED IN, SIR.

IF WE WANT TO FEEL AT HOME, WE HAVE TO START *RIGHT AWAY!*

ALIX, I'LL LET YOU UNPACK OUR LUGGAGE. I'M HEADING OVER TO MR. GOSSELIN'S OFFICE TO INTRODUCE MYSELF.

Visitor's Entrance

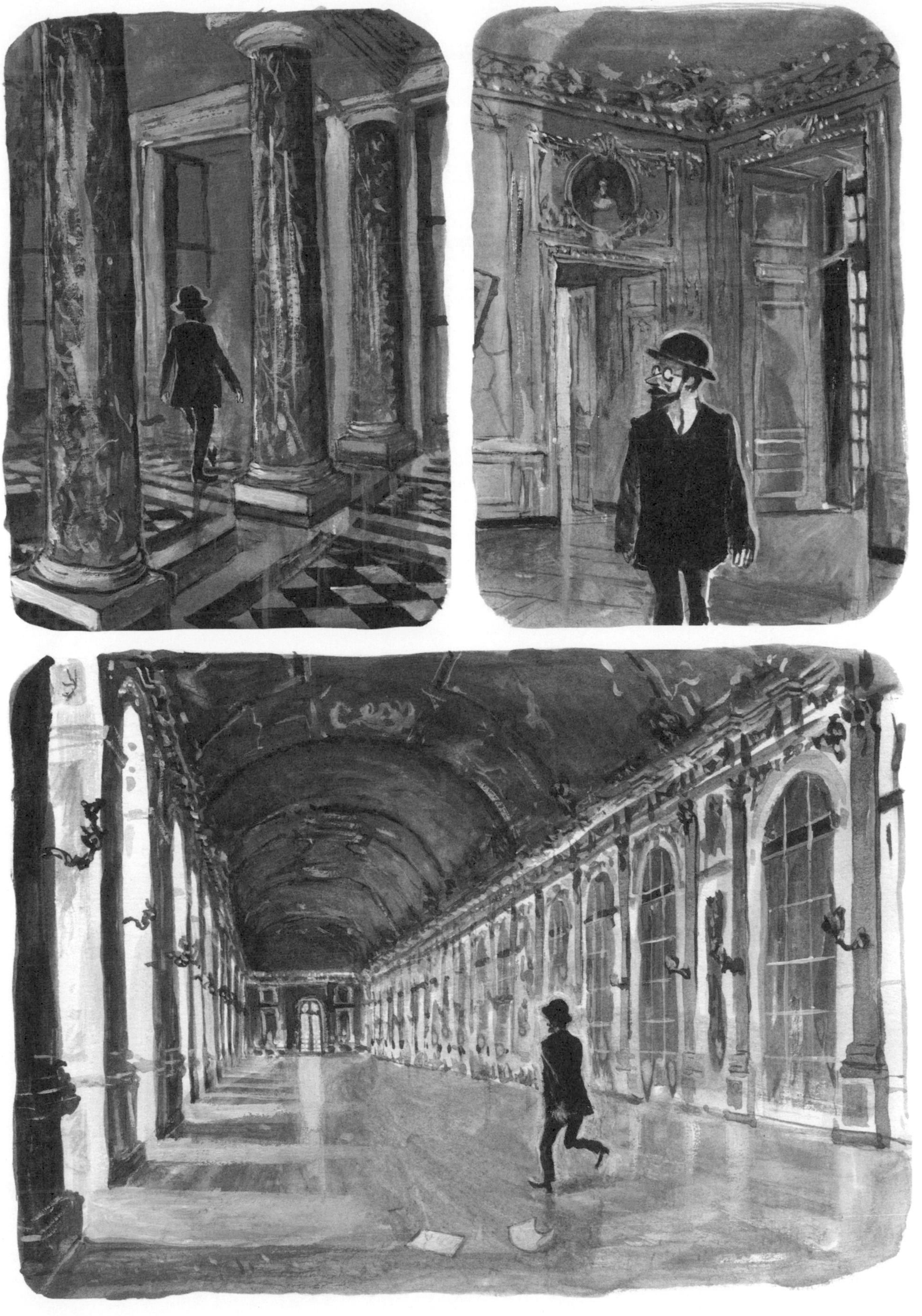

AH! YOU MUST BE *PIERRE DE NOLHAC.*

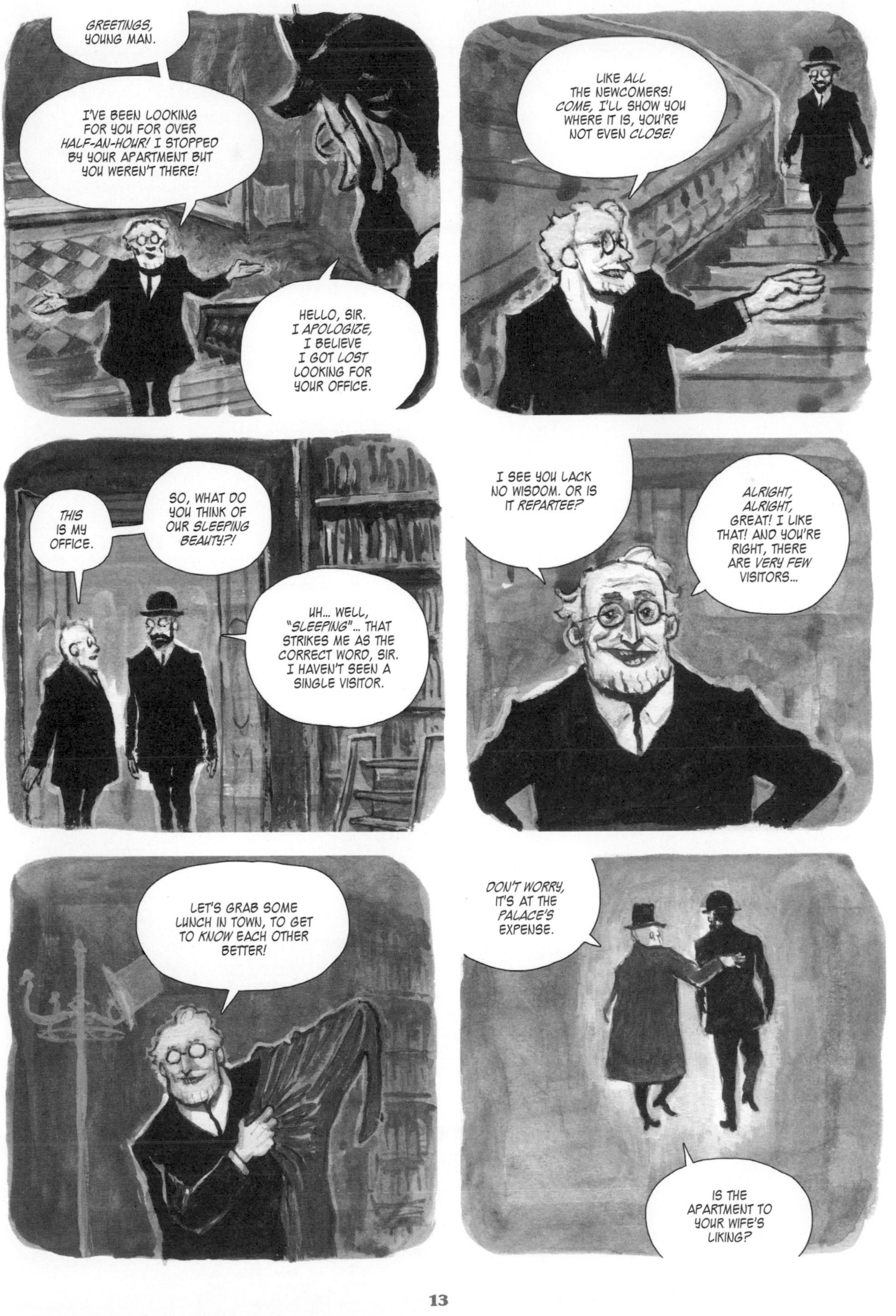
GREETINGS, YOUNG MAN.
I'VE BEEN LOOKING FOR YOU FOR OVER HALF-AN-HOUR! I STOPPED BY YOUR APARTMENT BUT YOU WEREN'T THERE!
HELLO, SIR. I APOLOGIZE, I BELIEVE I GOT LOST LOOKING FOR YOUR OFFICE.
LIKE ALL THE NEWCOMERS! COME, I'LL SHOW YOU WHERE IT IS, YOU'RE NOT EVEN CLOSE!
THIS IS MY OFFICE.
SO, WHAT DO YOU THINK OF OUR SLEEPING BEAUTY?!
UH... WELL, "SLEEPING"... THAT STRIKES ME AS THE CORRECT WORD, SIR. I HAVEN'T SEEN A SINGLE VISITOR.
I SEE YOU LACK NO WISDOM. OR IS IT REPARTEE?
ALRIGHT, ALRIGHT, GREAT! I LIKE THAT! AND YOU'RE RIGHT, THERE ARE VERY FEW VISITORS...
LET'S GRAB SOME LUNCH IN TOWN, TO GET TO KNOW EACH OTHER BETTER!
DON'T WORRY, IT'S AT THE PALACE'S EXPENSE.
IS THE APARTMENT TO YOUR WIFE'S LIKING?

MY FATHER WAS AS SURPRISED AS HE WAS AMAZED. HE HAD NEVER HAD A SUPERVISOR WHO CARED MORE ABOUT MAKING HIM FEEL COMFORTABLE THAN ABOUT LISTING HIS RESPONSIBILITIES.

SO, YOUNG MAN, HOW IN GOD'S NAME DID YOU END UP IN VERSAILLES?

I STUDIED PETRARCH* AT THE ÉCOLE FRANÇAISE DE ROME FOR A LONG TIME. AFTER RETURNING FROM ITALY, I DID AN INTERNSHIP AT THE NATIONAL LIBRARY.

I TOOK AN EXAM THERE FOR AN ATTACHÉ POSITION BUT THERE WERE MANY CANDIDATES COMPETING FOR THE ONLY SPOT AVAILABLE.

MHM. THAT'S WHAT I *THOUGHT*-- VERSAILLES COULD *ONLY* HAVE BEEN A *SECOND* CHOICE...

I'D CALL IT AN *UNEXPECTED* OPPORTUNITY.

MY FATHER HAD NO CHOICE BUT TO HALF-ADMIT TO HIS FAILURE. GABRIEL MONOD, A HISTORIAN WHO TAUGHT AT THE ÉCOLE DES HAUTES ÉTUDES, HAD ENCOURAGED HIM TO APPLY TO VERSAILLES. HE HAD ALSO FELT THAT THE AIR IN VERSAILLES WOULD BE HEALTHIER FOR ME AND MY BROTHERS.

*PETRARCH (1304-1374) WAS AN ITALIAN POET AND HUMANIST, WHO, TOGETHER WITH DANTE, WAS AT THE ORIGIN OF THE MODERN ITALIAN LANGUAGE.

PERFECT, HERE COMES OUR MEAL!

I CAN'T WAIT TO GET STARTED!

NOW, YOU MUSTN'T GET *TOO* EXCITED, YOUNG MAN! I AM *WELL AWARE* OF THE TREASURES UP THERE IN THE PALACE'S ATTICS.

BUT WE *MUSTN'T* REVEAL THEIR EXISTENCE!

OUR TASK IS TO *PRESERVE* THEM...

...WHICH IS ALL THE MORE EASY CONSIDERING THEY PRESERVE THEMSELVES.

YOU CAN READ, AND EVEN *WRITE*, BOOKS *ABOUT* VERSAILLES IF YOU LIKE, BUT LET'S LEAVE THIS MUSEUM IN PEACE--NO ONE IS INTERESTED IN IT ANYMORE IN THESE REPUBLICAN TIMES.

SO, TELL ME, DID YOU GET TO SEE MR. EIFFEL'S NEW CONSTRUCTION SITE?!

OF COURSE! THAT'S ALL THEY TALK ABOUT IN THE CAPITAL. THE PARISIANS ARE VERY *WORRIED*, FOR THAT MATTER...

IN THE FOLLOWING DAYS, MY FATHER LET EUGÈNE SHOW HIM AROUND. HE DIDN'T WANT HIS SUPERVISOR TO RUN INTO HIM LOST IN THE BIG PALACE AGAIN.

THE GALLERY OF GREAT BATTLES!

MR. GOSSELIN TOLD ME THAT IT WAS INSTALLED BY THE LAST KING OF FRANCE, A CERTAIN LOUIS-PHILIPPE...

...NOT THAT LONG AGO, AS A MATTER OF FACT, MR. DE NOLHAC!

SO I'VE BEEN TOLD.

FOLLOW ME, MR. DE NOLHAC, I'LL SHOW YOU HOW TO GET THERE WITHOUT HAVING TO GO BACK DOWN.

I'M RIGHT BEHIND YOU, EUGÈNE!

SEE? IT'S A SHORTCUT!

YOU HAVE DIRECT ACCESS TO THE CURATORIAL AREA FROM HERE.

HERE'S YOUR OFFICE! MR. GOSSELIN'S IS JUST ABOVE. I HEAR IT'S A LOT MESSIER THAN YOURS.

THANK YOU, EUGÈNE, THIS IS PERFECT.

WE'LL CONTINUE THE VISIT TOMORROW. I'M GOING TO GET TO WORK.

CONDITION OF THE MINISTERS' APARTMENTS

FOLLOWING CHARLES GOSSELIN'S
RECOMMENDATIONS DOWN TO
THE LETTER, MY FATHER BEGAN
TO IMMERSE HIMSELF IN THE
HISTORY OF VERSAILLES AS
SOON AS HE SETTLED IN.

IN PARTICULAR, HE HAD FUN GOING THROUGH
THE ARCHIVES TO SEE WHO HAD STAYED IN
OUR APARTMENT BEFORE US.

I WOULD FALL ASLEEP EVERY
NIGHT IMAGINING THAT THE KING HAD
PERHAPS SLEPT THERE TOO.

THE NEXT DAY.

I'LL WAKE THE BOYS UP AS SOON AS I'M READY.

GOOD, WE DON'T WANT THEM TO BE *LATE* FOR THEIR FIRST DAY OF SCHOOL HERE.

FIRST IMPRESSIONS ARE *ESSENTIAL!*

YOU KNOW SOMETHING ABOUT THAT, *MR. CONSERVATION ATTACHÉ.*

AT LEAST *THEY* WON'T GET *LOST* ON THE WAY...

RIGHT... I'D RATHER THEY DO AS I *SAY* AND NOT WHAT I *DO!*

ALRIGHT, EUGÈNE MUST BE WAITING ALREADY.

WHAT'S ON YOUR AGENDA FOR TODAY?

MRS. DU BARRY'S APARTMENTS UNDER THE ROOFS. YOU'LL *NEVER* GUESS WHAT CHARLES GOSSELIN TOLD ME: AN ADMINISTRATOR OF THE *NATIONAL ASSEMBLY* IS LIVING IN ONE WITH HIS WIFE AND CHILDREN...

A FEW HOURS LATER...

SO, HOW ARE THESE TOURS WITH EUGÈNE?

MOST INSTRUCTIVE! BUT HOW IS IT THAT HE KNOWS THE PALACE SO WELL AT HIS AGE?

HIS FATHER IS ALSO ONE OF OUR CUSTODIANS, AND HIS MOTHER RUNS A SMALL REFRESHMENT KIOSK NEAR THE GRAND CANAL.

HE WAS PRACTICALLY BORN HERE!

BY THE WAY, NOW THAT I THINK OF IT, BE WARY OF ALFRED LECLERC, THE ARCHITECT, AND GUSTAVE POISSON, THE MANAGER, WHO ALSO SERVES AS CHIEF OF STAFF.

VERY WELL.

THEY ONLY DO AS THEY PLEASE AND CARRY OUT HISTORICALLY INACCURATE WORK WITHOUT EVEN INFORMING ME!

ANYWAY, IT IS MY DUTY TO WARN YOU.

IN FACT, FROM NOW ON, YOU WILL BE IN CHARGE OF REPORTING TO THE MINISTRY. BE COURTEOUS, BUT NEVER FAIL TO MENTION ANY OF THEIR SHORTCOMINGS.

MY STUDIO AWAITS ME. I AM HAVING A LOT OF TROUBLE MAKING THE FINISHING TOUCHES ON A PAINTING.

MY FATHER WAS GRADUALLY DISCOVERING THIS NEW REALITY THROUGH WHICH HE WOULD SURELY HAVE TO ELBOW HIS WAY TO SUCCEED.

APRIL 1888.

SIX MONTHS PASSED SINCE WE HAD ARRIVED. THURSDAY WAS OUR FAVORITE DAY OF THE WEEK BECAUSE WE HAD OFF FROM SCHOOL. WHENEVER WE COULD, MY BROTHER AND I INSISTED ON ACCOMPANYING MY FATHER TO THE STATION. WE WERE FASCINATED WITH THE SMOKING MACHINERY THAT LOADED AND UNLOADED PASSENGERS.

WATCH OUT FOR THE TRAIN, BOYS!

WHEN WILL YOU BE BACK, FATHER?

THIS AFTERNOON. I HAVE A *VERY* IMPORTANT LUNCH MEETING IN PARIS.

I'LL BE BACK BEFORE YOU KNOW IT.

IN THE MEANTIME, YOU GET TO HAVE FUN WITH PAOLO AND FRANÇOIS.

MY FATHER WAS MEETING WITH PHILIPPE GILLE, CRITIC AT *LE FIGARO* AND PIERRE PUVIS DE CHAVANNE, ONE OF THE GREAT SYMBOLIST PAINTERS OF THE LATE CENTURY. HE WAS BEGINNING TO FORM WHAT HE WOULD LATER MOCKINGLY CALL HIS "PARISIAN STREAMER," A NETWORK OF CELEBRITIES INTERTWINED LIKE RIBBONS AT MARDI GRAS.

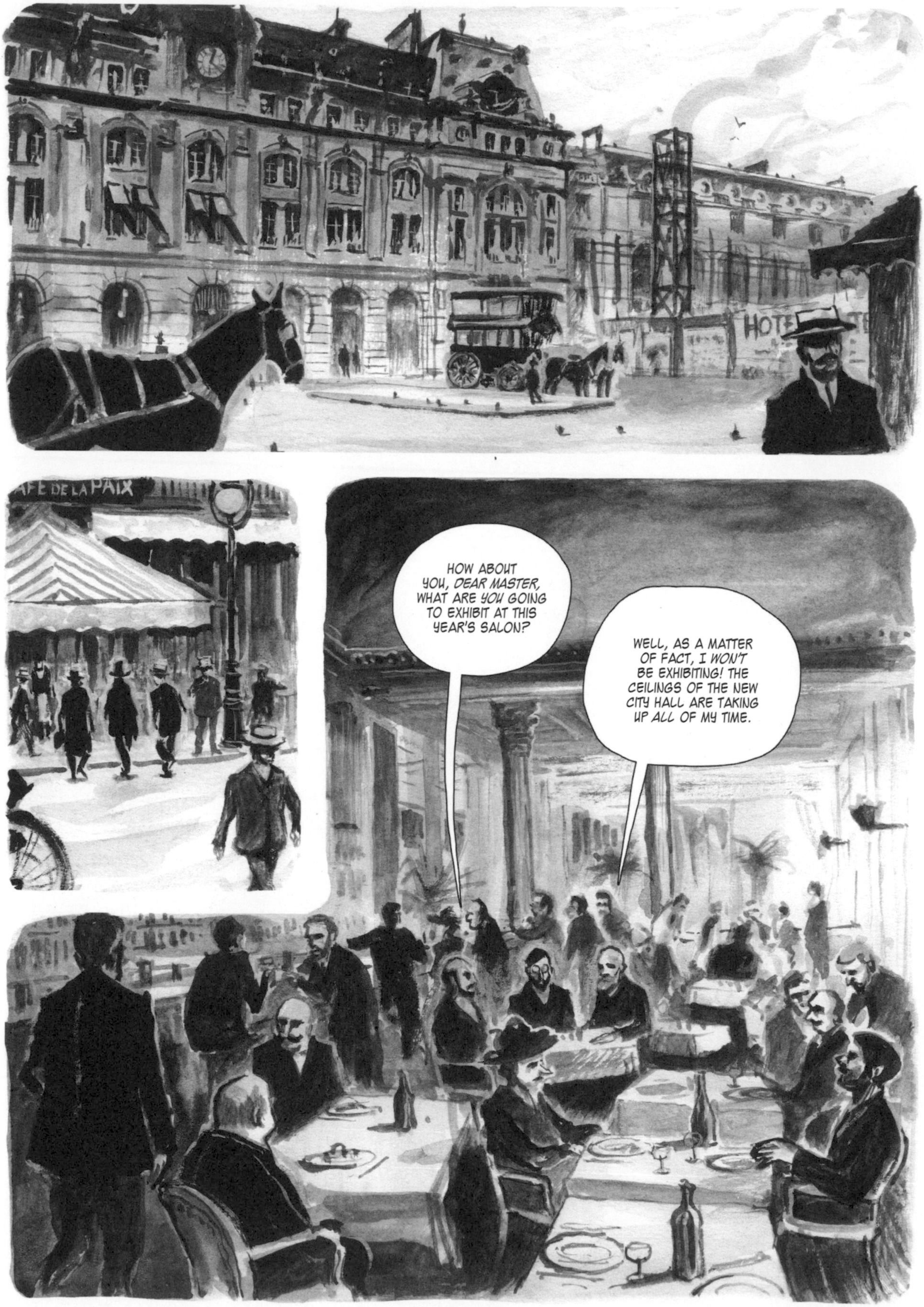
HOW ABOUT YOU, *DEAR MASTER,* WHAT ARE *YOU* GOING TO EXHIBIT AT THIS YEAR'S SALON?
WELL, AS A MATTER OF FACT, I *WON'T* BE EXHIBITING! THE CEILINGS OF THE NEW CITY HALL ARE TAKING UP *ALL* OF MY TIME.

THE COMMUNE* DID INDEED CAUSE A LOT OF DESTRUCTION IN PARIS. FORTUNATELY, VERSAILLES WAS SPARED!

PERHAPS, BUT IT WASN'T SPARED FROM *TIME ITSELF.* UNFORTUNATELY, THERE IS LITTLE LEFT TO ADMIRE SINCE LOUIS-PHILIPPE'S WORK AND THE PRUSSIAN OCCUPATION.

SO, YOU HAVE A LOT OF *FREE TIME?*

MAKE NO MISTAKE, I AM *HARD AT WORK* EXAMINING THE ARCHIVES TO STUDY THE LIVES THE MONARCHS LED THERE.

FOR SEVERAL MONTHS NOW, I HAVE BEEN TAKING A CLOSE INTEREST IN MARIE-ANTOINETTE. I THINK I'VE EVEN MADE SOME INTERESTING *DISCOVERIES.*

YOU *PUZZLE* ME, DE NOLHAC. YOU DON'T SEEM TO *REALIZE* YOU'RE LIVING AMONG *MASTERPIECES* OF FRENCH ART.

IT'S A GREAT *PITY.* EXAMINE THEM MORE CAREFULLY AND TRY TO UNDERSTAND THEM, STARTING WITH THE CEILINGS, FOR EXAMPLE! NEVER *LIMIT* YOURSELF IN YOUR WORK, *ESPECIALLY* NOT IN VERSAILLES.

I'D ACTUALLY LOVE TO GO BACK... AND AUGUSTE RODIN IS DYING TO SEE THE STATUES IN THE GARDENS AGAIN. PERHAPS WE COULD COME TOGETHER. IT'S PARADISE FOR A SCULPTOR AS TALENTED AS HE!

I WOULD BE *DELIGHTED* TO WELCOME YOU.

*THE PARIS COMMUNE WAS A RADICAL SOCIALIST AND REVOLUTIONARY GOVERNMENT THAT RULED PARIS FROM MARCH 18 TO MAY 28, 1871. THE FRANCO-PRUSSIAN WAR HAD LED TO THE CAPTURE OF EMPEROR NAPOLEON III IN SEPTEMBER 1870, THE COLLAPSE OF THE SECOND FRENCH EMPIRE, AND THE BEGINNING OF THE THIRD REPUBLIC.

PALACE LIFE HAD BECOME OUR DAILY LIFE.

AS OUR IMAGINATIONS TOOK US ON ADVENTURES THROUGHOUT THE PARK, OUR FAMILY GOT A LITTLE BIGGER WITH FRÉDÉRIC, MY NEW LITTLE BROTHER. FOUR BOYS!

MY FATHER, WHO COULD NOT GET THE WORDS OF PUVIS DE CHAVANNE OUT OF HIS HEAD, HAD CHANGED HIS STRATEGY.

HE WOULDN'T BE SATISFIED WITH JUST EXPLORING HISTORY. HIS MAIN MISSION, AFTER ALL, WAS TO EXPLORE THE COLLECTIONS, WHETHER CHARLES GOSSELIN LIKED IT OR NOT.

JULY 1889.

HELLO, MR. FRANCE, IT IS AN *HONOR* FOR ME TO WELCOME YOU TO VERSAILLES.

PLEASE EXCUSE MR. GOSSELIN, HE *COULDN'T* MAKE IT.

HELLO, MY FRIEND!

PARIS-VERSAILLES IS *QUITE A TRIP!*

THAT'S TRUE, BUT THE RAILWAY IS STILL MORE CONVENIENT THAN THE HOURS IT TOOK THE KING TO REACH THE CAPITAL IN A *HORSE-DRAWN CARRIAGE.*

SO, *THIS* IS WHERE THE QUEEN PLAYED *SHEPHERDESS?*

AND WHERE SHE COULD BE FREE FROM THE COURT'S ETIQUETTE! SHE WAS A *FASCINATING* PERSON, MUCH MORE *MODERN* THAN WE MIGHT *THINK.*

NO KIDDING! A QUEEN WHO LET THE FINANCIERS STARVE HER PEOPLE... PUBLISH A BOOK TO HER GLORY THE YEAR WE CELEBRATE THE HUNDREDTH ANNIVERSARY OF THE FRENCH REVOLUTION, AND YOU MAY VERY WELL END UP LIKE *SHE* DID!

25

MARIE-ANTOINETTE, JUST LIKE VERSAILLES, SUFFERS FROM HER POOR REPUTATION. IS THE FRENCH REPUBLIC NOT STABLE ENOUGH TO MAKE PEACE WITH ITS ROYAL PAST NOW?

YOU'RE PREACHING TO THE CHOIR! I'LL REMIND YOU THAT MY WIFE IS A *DIRECT DESCENDANT* OF ONE OF LOUIS XVI'S PAINTERS!

AND HOW DO YOU PLAN TO RESTORE THE PREMISES?

I HAVE NO IDEA, TO BE HONEST... VERSAILLES GETS VERY LITTLE SUPPORT FROM THE MINISTRY.

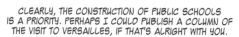

CLEARLY, THE CONSTRUCTION OF PUBLIC SCHOOLS IS A PRIORITY. PERHAPS I COULD PUBLISH A COLUMN OF THE VISIT TO VERSAILLES, IF THAT'S ALRIGHT WITH YOU.

THE PRESS HAS A VOICE THAT *CARRIES*...

I WOULD BE VERY GRATEFUL TO YOU, MR. FRANCE. PUBLIC SUPPORT FROM A MAN OF YOUR STATURE WOULD MEAN A LOT.

PLEASE, IT'S NOTHING AT ALL. AND YOU KNOW, I LIKE NON-CONFORMITY.

SEND ME A COPY OF YOUR BOOK ON MARIE-ANTOINETTE WHEN IT'S READY! I WOULD LOVE TO READ IT.

I'LL MAKE SURE OF IT. IT'LL BE AVAILABLE THIS FALL.

AND I'M ALREADY WORKING ON A SECOND BOOK.

THE ARDOR OF YOUTH! YOU KNOW WHAT ARISTOTLE SAID?

"THE MORE YOU KNOW, THE MORE YOU REALIZE YOU DON'T KNOW." BE CAREFUL NOT TO GET LOST IN YOUR WORK. I'LL BE BACK TO SEE YOU, DE NOLHAC. AND SAY HELLO TO CHARLES GOSSELIN FOR ME. I'LL BET HE'S IN HIS STUDIO, PER USUAL!

SUMMER OF 1890.

PIERRE!

AH, I SEE YOU STILL HAVE YOUR NOSE IN YOUR BOOKS...

I'M HAVING LUNCH WITH THE MAYOR AND HIS WIFE AT THE LIMOUSIN AT ONE O'CLOCK SHARP... WILL YOU JOIN ME?

UH... YES, OF COURSE. I'M IN A HURRY, I'D LIKE TO FINISH CORRECTING THIS FILE TO SEND TO PARIS TOMORROW MORNING.

YOU ALWAYS HAVE TO OVERDO EVERYTHING!

I HOPE ONE DAY YOU COME TO UNDERSTAND THAT THE ADMINISTRATION WILL NEVER GIVE YOU ITS SUPPORT. THEY WON'T EVEN BOTHER TAKING THE TRAIN TO COME SEE US...

YES, YES, I KNOW... I'LL MEET UP WITH YOU LATER BECAUSE I ALSO PROMISED ALIX I'D STOP BY BEFORE LUNCH. FRÉDÉRIC ISN'T GETTING ANY BETTER.

... I SEE. PLEASE EXTEND MY RESPECTS AND SUPPORT TO YOUR WIFE.

FOR SEVERAL WEEKS NOW, MY LITTLE BROTHER, FRÉDÉRIC, THE FIRST DE NOLHAC TO BE BORN AT THE PALACE, HAD BEEN SUFFERING FROM A LUNG INFECTION. HE WAS BEDRIDDEN.

ALIX?

HOW IS HE?

I JUST PUT HIM TO BED, HIS MOANING IS GETTING LOUDER AND LOUDER. I THINK WE SHOULD GET THE DOCTOR TO COME BACK.

CAN'T YOU PUT VERSAILLES ASIDE FOR JUST A FEW HOURS?!

I'LL GO SEE HIM LATER TODAY, GET SOME REST IN THE MEANTIME. I HAVE TO MEET CHARLES FOR LUNCH.

THE PALACE HAS BEEN STANDING FOR *TWO CENTURIES*, IT ISN'T GOING TO COLLAPSE!

I'LL BE BACK SOON. BE STRONG, ALIX.

WE'LL ALL PRAY FOR HIM TONIGHT.

THAT EVENING, AT DINNER...

I WAS OLD ENOUGH TO UNDERSTAND THE TRAGEDY THAT WAS PLAYING OUT IN THE NEXT ROOM, BUT TOO YOUNG TO GRASP THE SIGNIFICANCE OF MY MOTHER'S SILENCE.

AND HOW WAS SCHOOL TODAY, PAOLO AND HENRI?

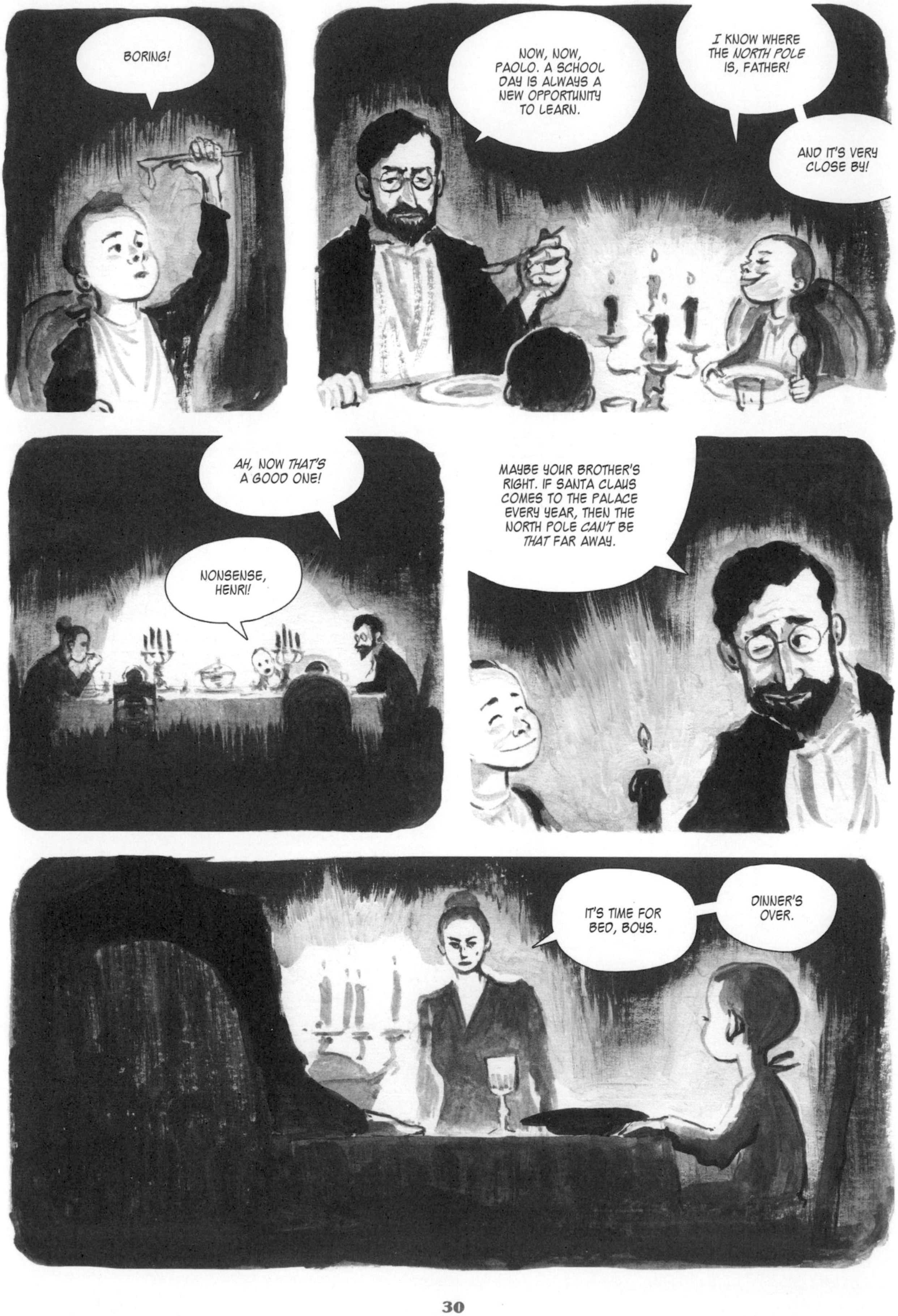
BORING!
NOW, NOW, PAOLO. A SCHOOL DAY IS ALWAYS A NEW OPPORTUNITY TO LEARN.
I KNOW WHERE THE *NORTH POLE* IS, FATHER!
AND IT'S VERY CLOSE BY!
AH, NOW *THAT'S* A GOOD ONE!
NONSENSE, HENRI!
MAYBE YOUR BROTHER'S RIGHT. IF SANTA CLAUS COMES TO THE PALACE EVERY YEAR, THEN THE NORTH POLE *CAN'T* BE *THAT* FAR AWAY.
IT'S TIME FOR BED, BOYS.
DINNER'S OVER.

YOUR MOTHER'S RIGHT, OFF TO BED.

AS FOR ME, I HAVE TO GET BACK TO A PENDING MATTER. I'M GOING BACK TO MY OFFICE FOR A WHILE.

BRUSH YOUR TEETH. I'LL COME READ YOU A STORY, BOYS.

SO THIS IS OUR LIFE NOW: YOU, ME, AND THE PALACE IN BETWEEN!

DON'T GET IT TWISTED, ALIX. I'M JUST AS CONCERNED ABOUT FRÉDÉRIC'S HEALTH AS YOU ARE.

BUT WHAT MORE CAN WE DO?

YOU COULD STAY WITH HIM INSTEAD OF SPENDING ALL YOUR TIME IN THAT OFFICE OR AT THESE SUPPOSEDLY "IMPORTANT" MEETINGS.

ARE YOU THE ONLY ONE WHO DOESN'T REALIZE THAT VERSAILLES IS A THING OF THE PAST?

PARIS, 3 RUE DE VALOIS. FEBRUARY 1891.

HELLO, SIR, I'M HERE TO SEE THE SUB-DIRECTOR OF THE BEAUX-ARTS.

GREETINGS, SIR, AND YOU ARE?

AFTER MY LITTLE BROTHER DIED, LIFE EVENTUALLY RETURNED TO NORMAL.

A FEW MONTHS LATER, MY FATHER RECEIVED AN UNEXPECTED INVITATION TO THE SUB-DIRECTORATE OF THE BEAUX-ARTS IN PARIS. COULD THIS MEAN THEY WERE FINALLY INTERESTED IN VERSAILLES?

PIERRE DE NOLHAC, CONSERVATION ATTACHÉ AT THE PALACE OF VERSAILLES.

VERY WELL. MR. DEPUTY DIRECTOR, GUSTAVE LARROUMET, WILL SEE YOU NOW.

PLEASE GIVE ME A MOMENT, I'LL ANNOUNCE YOUR PRESENCE.

MR. PIERRE DE NOLHAC.

THANK YOU. COME IN, MR. DE NOLHAC.

HAVE A SEAT.

THIS IS PAUL SIMON, FROM THE MINISTRY OF FOREIGN AFFAIRS.

I ASKED TO SEE YOU TO ENTRUST YOU WITH A DIPLOMATIC MISSION. YOU'RE NOT SUPPOSED TO KNOW THIS, BUT EMPRESS FREDERICK, DAUGHTER OF QUEEN VICTORIA AND MOTHER OF THE GERMAN EMPEROR WILHELM II, IS ON A PRIVATE TRIP TO FRANCE RIGHT NOW...

...AND SHE *INSISTS* ON VISITING VERSAILLES THIS THURSDAY.

SURELY YOU UNDERSTAND, SIR, THE *DELICATE* NATURE OF THE SITUATION FOR THE QUAI D'ORSAY AND FRANCE.

*NATIONALIST AND MILITARISTIC POLITICAL MOVEMENT OF THE LATE NINETEENTH CENTURY THAT ALMOST BROUGHT ABOUT THE COLLAPSE OF THE THIRD REPUBLIC. BOULANGISM TOOK ITS NAME FROM ITS LEADER, GENERAL GEORGES BOULANGER.

VERSAILLES. THE MORNING OF THURSDAY, FEBRUARY 19, 1891.

IN 1871, AT THE END OF THE WAR, CHANCELLOR BISMARCK HAD HAD THE INSOLENCE TO PROCLAIM THE GERMAN EMPIRE IN THE HALL OF MIRRORS, A FINAL INSULT TO FRANCE, WHICH HAD BEEN DEFEATED BY THE PRUSSIANS.

IT WOULD'VE BEEN DIFFICULT FOR THE VENGEFUL FRENCH POPULATION TO TOLERATE A GERMAN EMPRESS STROLLING AROUND THE VERY SITE OF NATIONAL HUMILIATION LIKE A TOURIST, REMEMBERING "THE GOOD OL' DAYS."

GREETINGS, YOUR HIGHNESS.

WELCOME TO VERSAILLES. I WILL BE GUIDING YOU THROUGH THE KING'S STATE APARTMENT TODAY.

SO *YOU* ARE THE YOUNG MAN WHO HAS BEEN CHOSEN TO BE MY CHAPERONE.

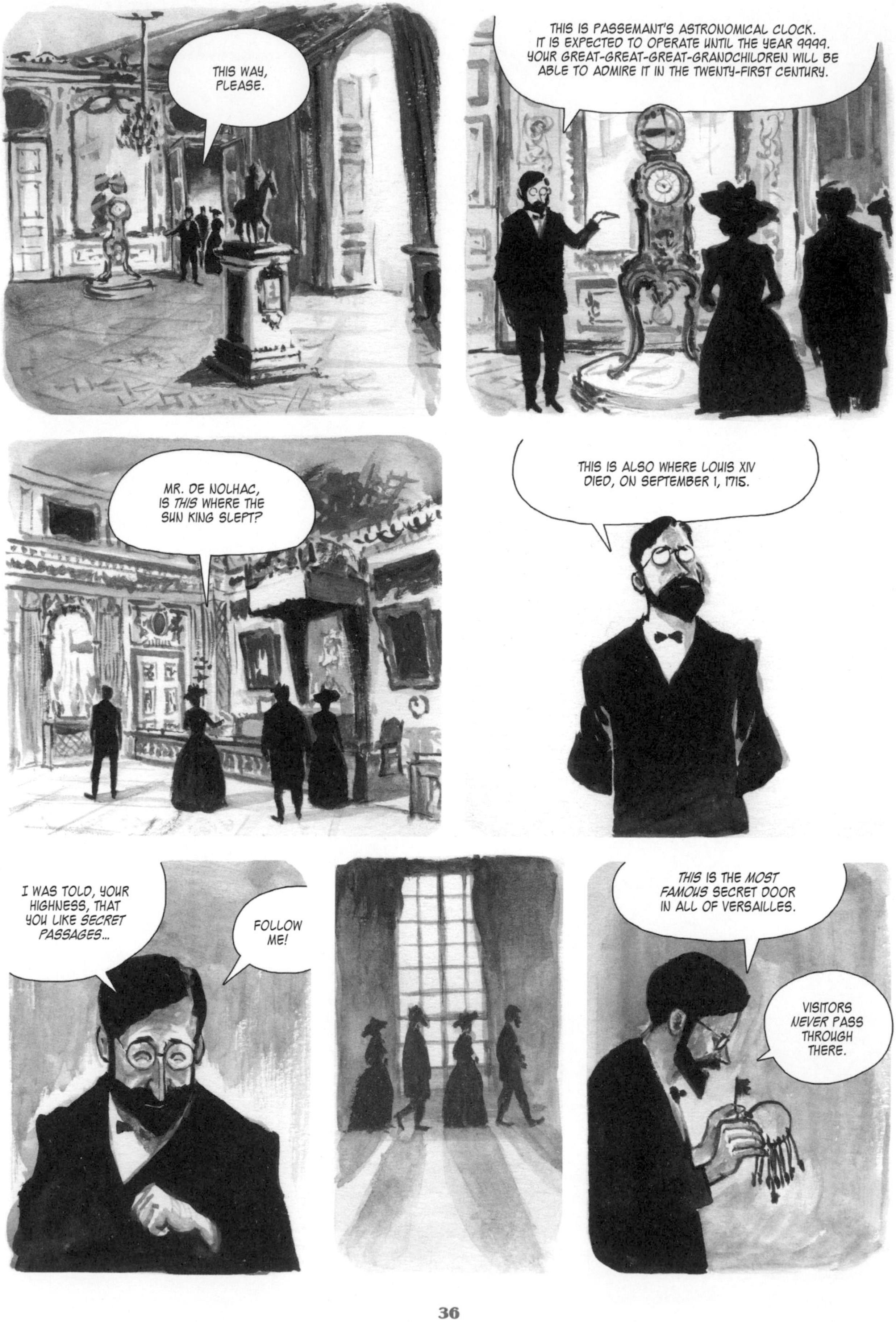
THIS WAY, PLEASE.
THIS IS PASSEMANT'S ASTRONOMICAL CLOCK. IT IS EXPECTED TO OPERATE UNTIL THE YEAR 9999. YOUR GREAT-GREAT-GREAT-GRANDCHILDREN WILL BE ABLE TO ADMIRE IT IN THE TWENTY-FIRST CENTURY.
MR. DE NOLHAC, IS *THIS* WHERE THE SUN KING SLEPT?
THIS IS ALSO WHERE LOUIS XIV DIED, ON SEPTEMBER 1, 1715.
I WAS TOLD, YOUR HIGHNESS, THAT YOU LIKE *SECRET PASSAGES*...
FOLLOW ME!
THIS IS THE *MOST FAMOUS* SECRET DOOR IN ALL OF VERSAILLES.
VISITORS *NEVER* PASS THROUGH THERE.

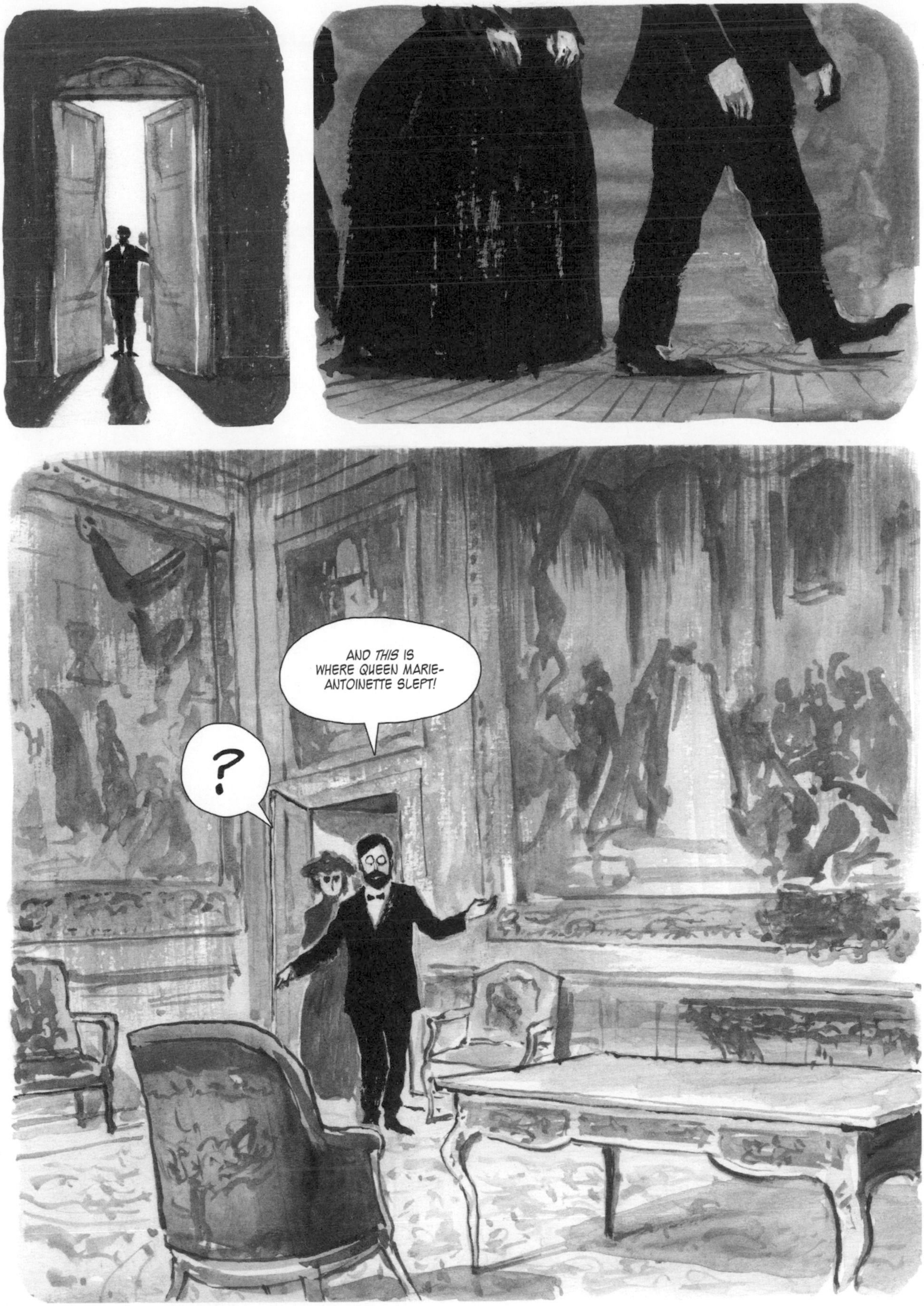
?
AND *THIS* IS WHERE QUEEN MARIE-ANTOINETTE SLEPT!

IT'S HARD TO IMAGINE THAT MARIE-ANTOINETTE SLEPT HERE!

THERE'S NO BED!

YET, THIS IS WHERE SHE SPENT HER NIGHTS. WHEN SHE WASN'T IN HER PETIT TRIANON.

AND IT WAS THROUGH THIS PASSAGE THAT SHE JOINED LOUIS XVI WHEN THE REVOLUTIONARIES REACHED THE PALACE GATES.

THE PIECES OF FURNITURE WERE ALL DISPERSED DURING THE FRENCH REVOLUTION. THERE ARE VERY FEW TRACES OF THE QUEEN'S FURNITURE.

MR. DE NOLHAC!

I APOLOGIZE, YOUR HIGHNESS, AN URGENT MATTER HAS COME UP.

I SUGGEST YOU ENJOY THE HALL OF MIRRORS. YOU WILL FIND IT RIGHT AFTER THE PEACE ROOM.

PERFECT, EUGÈNE, I'LL WAIT FOR YOU OUTSIDE AS PLANNED.

THIS WAY, PLEASE, YOUR HIGHNESS...

THE CONSERVATION ATTACHÉ WILL JOIN US OUTSIDE IN A FEW MOMENTS.

THANK YOU FOR THIS WONDERFUL VISIT. THIS PALACE IS *FULL* OF SURPRISES...

IT WORKED, MR. DE NOLHAC!

YES, THANK YOU, EUGÈNE! I WANTED TO AVOID BEING SEEN ALONGSIDE THE EMPRESS IN THE SYMBOLIC HALL OF MIRRORS AT ALL COSTS.

IT WAS A MISSION ACCOMPLISHED FOR MY FATHER: HE HAD MANAGED TO BE COURTEOUS WITHOUT SMEARING FRANCE'S HONOR. HE WAS A PATRIOT, AND DID NOT APPROVE OF THE GERMANS RETURNING TO VERSAILLES, EVEN FOR LEISURE. HE DIDN'T KNOW IT YET, BUT HIS ACHIEVEMENT WOULD BE REWARDED.

A FEW WEEKS LATER, MY FATHER DEFENDED HIS DOCTORAL THESIS AT THE SORBONNE, IN THE GRAND AMPHITHÉÂTRE INAUGURATED TWO YEARS EARLIER, IN 1889.

AS HE ELOQUENTLY CONCLUDED HIS PRESENTATION ON PETRARCH, ONE OF THE JURY MEMBERS SPOKE.

FIRST OF ALL, SIR, I CANNOT FORGET THAT, AS A DOCTORAL STUDENT, YOU BELONG TO MY ADMINISTRATION. YOU HAVE CARRIED OUT A SERVICE ON A DIFFICULT AND *DANGEROUS* DAY FOR THE COUNTRY, AND THE GOVERNMENT WILL FIND IT APPROPRIATE THAT I TAKE THIS OPPORTUNITY TO THANK YOU *PUBLICLY* FOR IT.

AT JUST THIRTY-TWO YEARS OF AGE, MY FATHER WAS HONORED FOR THE FIRST TIME BY THE SUB-DIRECTOR OF THE BEAUX-ARTS BEFORE AN AUDIENCE OF DISTINGUISHED INDIVIDUALS. BY THE ONE WHO HAD INITIALLY CONSIDERED HIM A "SIMPLE" ATTACHÉ.

MONDAY, OCTOBER 24, 1892, 6:30 IN THE MORNING.

EUGÈNE?!

WHAT'S GOING ON?

MR. DE NOLHAC, I THINK MR. GOSSELIN'S DEAD!

HE WON'T WAKE UP, HIS SON SENT ME!

Chapter 2
REDISCOVERING VERSAILLES

1892, A FEW DAYS BEFORE CHRISTMAS.

THAT'S *TERRIFIC*, PIERRE. YOU ARE *NOW* THE *CHIEF CURATOR* OF THE PALACE OF VERSAILLES. HOW FAR YOU'VE COME SINCE ROME!

YOU'LL SEE, ANDRÉ, ALIX HAS MADE A MARVEL OF OUR APARTMENT IN THE MINISTERS' WING. WE'RE MOVING OUT OF IT TODAY.

YOU'LL SEE, YOU'LL LIKE IT THERE.

FOLLOWING HIS APPOINTMENT, MY FATHER MOVED US TO THE PAVILLON DUFOUR, INTO THE GOSSELINS' FORMER APARTMENT. OUR FAMILY NOW INCLUDED FOUR CHILDREN, SINCE THE BIRTH OF MARIE-LOUISE THE PREVIOUS YEAR. AND A FIFTH WAS DUE.

WHERE SHOULD WE PUT THIS TRUNK, MR. CURATOR?

LEAVE IT IN THE ENTRANCE, MY WIFE WILL DECIDE LATER!

TO REPLACE HIM AS CONSERVATION ATTACHÉ, MY FATHER HAD CALLED ON HIS FRIEND, ANDRÉ PÉRATÉ, WHOM HE HAD MET AT THE ÉCOLE FRANÇAISE DE ROME.

I LOOK FORWARD TO GETTING TO WORK AND DISCOVERING THE PLACES YOU TOLD ME ABOUT IN YOUR LETTERS.

AFTER CHRISTMAS, ANDRÉ, AFTER CHRISTMAS... LET'S ALLOW OUR WIVES TO SETTLE IN AND OUR CHILDREN TO ENJOY THE HOLIDAYS!

AS ALIX LIKES TO REMIND ME, VERSAILLES CAN WAIT A FEW DAYS...

1892, CHRISTMAS MORNING.

FATHER! FATHER!

WHAT'S GOING ON, HENRI?

THE NORTH POLE, FATHER! THE NORTH POLE'S NEARBY! SANTA CLAUS MUST HAVE COME BY NOW!

I WONDER HOW HE GOT IN!

HE'S GOT SO MANY CHOICES, WITH ALL THE CHIMNEYS IN VERSAILLES!

THE ONE IN THE HALL OF MIRRORS!

THE ONE IN THE QUEEN'S ROOM!

BUT HENRI, THERE'S NO CHIMNEY IN THE GRAND GALLERY! I'D SAY THROUGH THE LIVING ROOM...

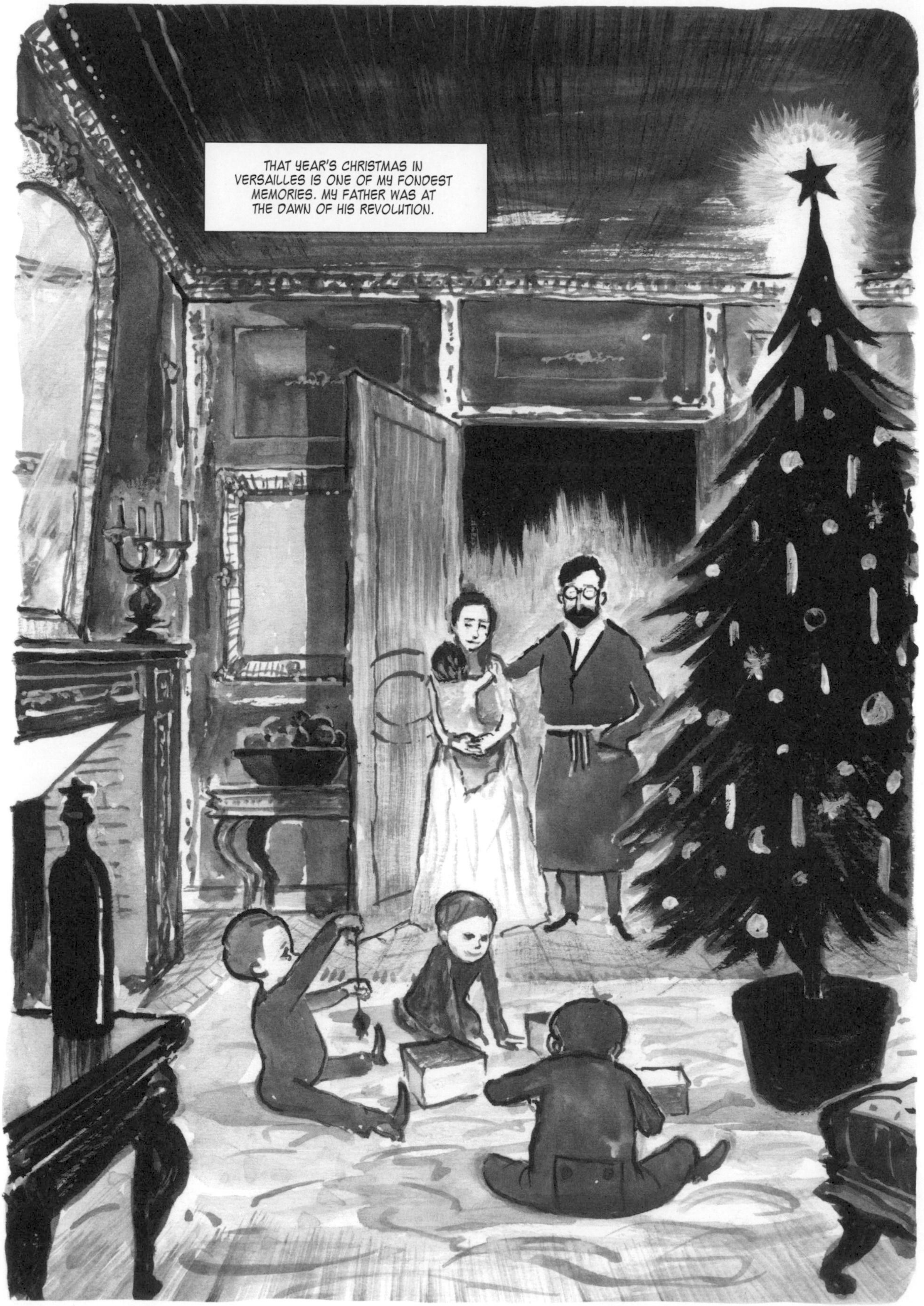
THAT YEAR'S CHRISTMAS IN VERSAILLES IS ONE OF MY FONDEST MEMORIES. MY FATHER WAS AT THE DAWN OF HIS REVOLUTION.

FEBRUARY 1893. MY FATHER'S OBJECTIVE WAS SIMPLE: TO CORRECT THE "MISTAKES" OF LOUIS-PHILIPPE WHO HAD THE PALACE TRANSFORMED INTO A MUSEUM OF FRENCH HISTORY,* NOTABLY BY PLACING THE MASTERPIECES OF THE *ANCIEN RÉGIME* IN THE ATTICS.

*IN 1837, THE PALACE OF VERSAILLES BECAME A MUSEUM DEDICATED "TO ALL THE GLORIES OF FRANCE," AIMING TO ESTABLISH THE LEGITIMACY OF LOUIS-PHILIPPE, WHO HAD BEEN PROCLAIMED KING OF THE FRENCH IN 1830. THE ROYAL COLLECTIONS WERE REPLACED BY PAINTINGS COMMISSIONED FROM ARTISTS OF THE TIME, ILLUSTRATING EVENTS OR CHARACTERS OF FRENCH HISTORY.

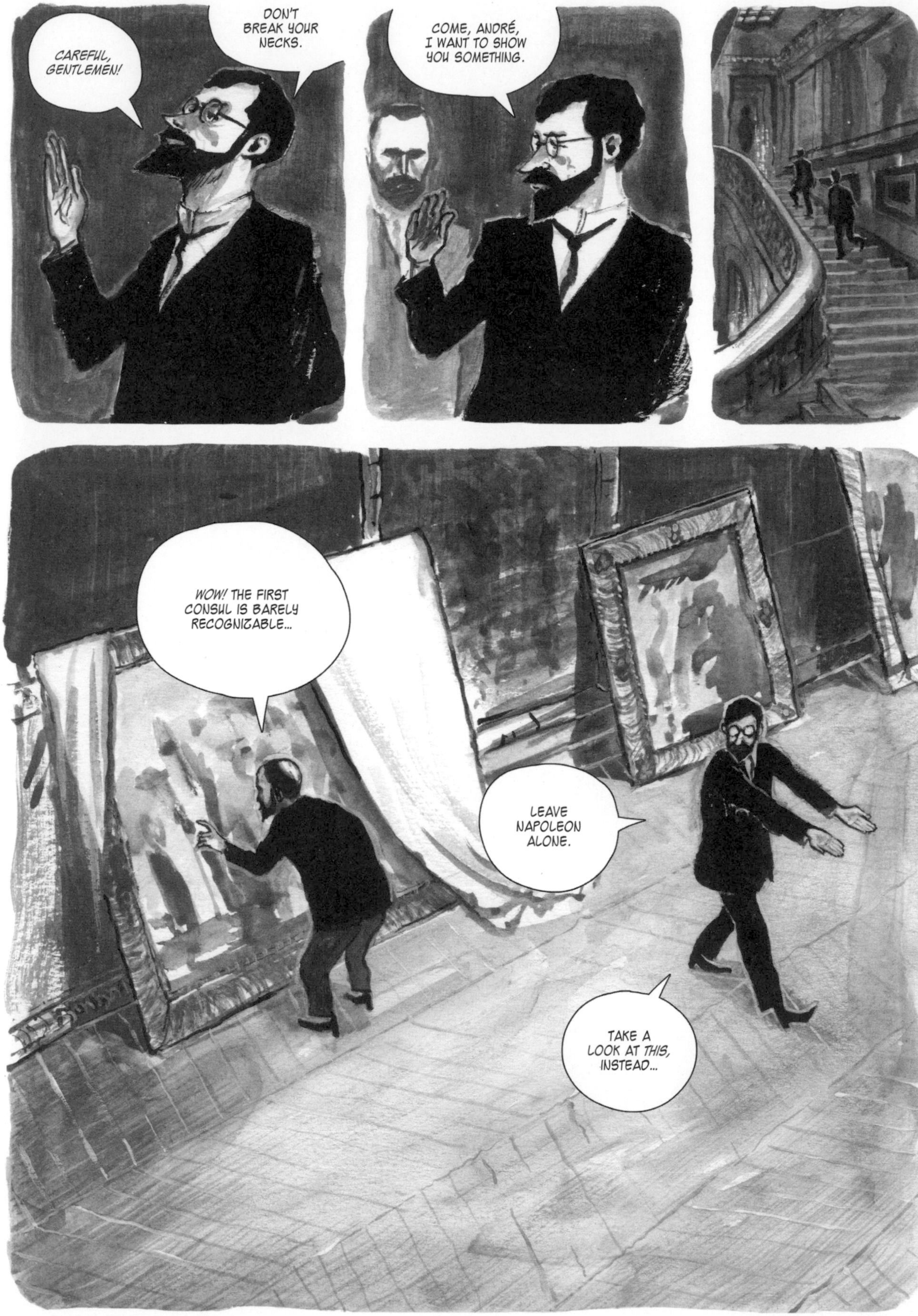
CAREFUL, GENTLEMEN!
DON'T BREAK YOUR NECKS.
COME, ANDRÉ, I WANT TO SHOW YOU SOMETHING.
WOW! THE FIRST CONSUL IS BARELY RECOGNIZABLE...
LEAVE NAPOLEON ALONE.
TAKE A LOOK AT THIS, INSTEAD...

VOILÀ: MADAME HENRIETTE!

IT'S A NATTIER, ANDRÉ!

I THOUGHT HIS PAINTINGS WERE LOST!

I CAN'T BELIEVE IT...

LOUIS XV'S DAUGHTER HASN'T AGED A BIT.

AND THERE ARE MANY MORE.

WE HAVE HERE ALL THE PORTRAITS OF LOUIS XV'S DAUGHTERS...

JEAN-MARC NATTIER WAS THE COURT'S PORTRAIT PAINTER.

ANDRÉ, WE MAY HAVE FOUND A WAY TO REVIVE VERSAILLES.

WHAT ARE YOU THINKING...?

AN EXHIBITION!

SURELY YOU AREN'T SERIOUS, DE NOLHAC!

PARIS, FRENCH NATIONAL MUSEUMS DIRECTORATE.

YOU'VE ALREADY PUT NEARLY ALL OF THE CUSTODIANS TO WORK IN THE STATE APARTMENTS REORGANIZING THE COLLECTIONS OR GOD KNOWS WHAT!

NOW, NOW, GENTLEMEN, PLEASE.

MR. DIRECTOR OF THE NATIONAL MUSEUMS, THE PALACE OF VERSAILLES CONTAINS MANY TREASURES THAT I WOULD LIKE TO BRING TO THE PUBLIC'S ATTENTION. THE PALACE HAS BEEN DORMANT FOR TOO LONG.

DUE TO HIS YOUNG AGE, AND PERHAPS HIS BOLDNESS, MY FATHER HAD TO FIGHT TO CARRY OUT HIS PROJECTS, DESPITE RESISTING FORCES. MARCEL LAMBERT, THE NEW ARCHITECT WHO HAD REPLACED ALFRED LECLERC, WASN'T WILLING TO APPEASE RELATIONS BETWEEN THE DEPARTMENTS ANY MORE THAN HIS PREDECESSOR WAS.

CERTAINLY, DE NOLHAC, BUT AS YOU KNOW, NO ADDITIONAL CREDIT CAN BE GRANTED TO YOU.

FURTHERMORE, MR. LAMBERT NEEDS TO HAVE ENOUGH STAFF TO CARRY OUT HIS *OWN* MISSIONS.

RIGHT, AS IT SO HAPPENS, ALL MY MEN ARE WORKING ON RENOVATING THE BUSTS IN THE MARBLE COURT AND REFURBISHING THE SOUTH WING.

BUT IF I ONLY USE THE MEANS *AT MY DISPOSAL*, DO I HAVE YOUR *CONSENT*, MR. DIRECTOR?

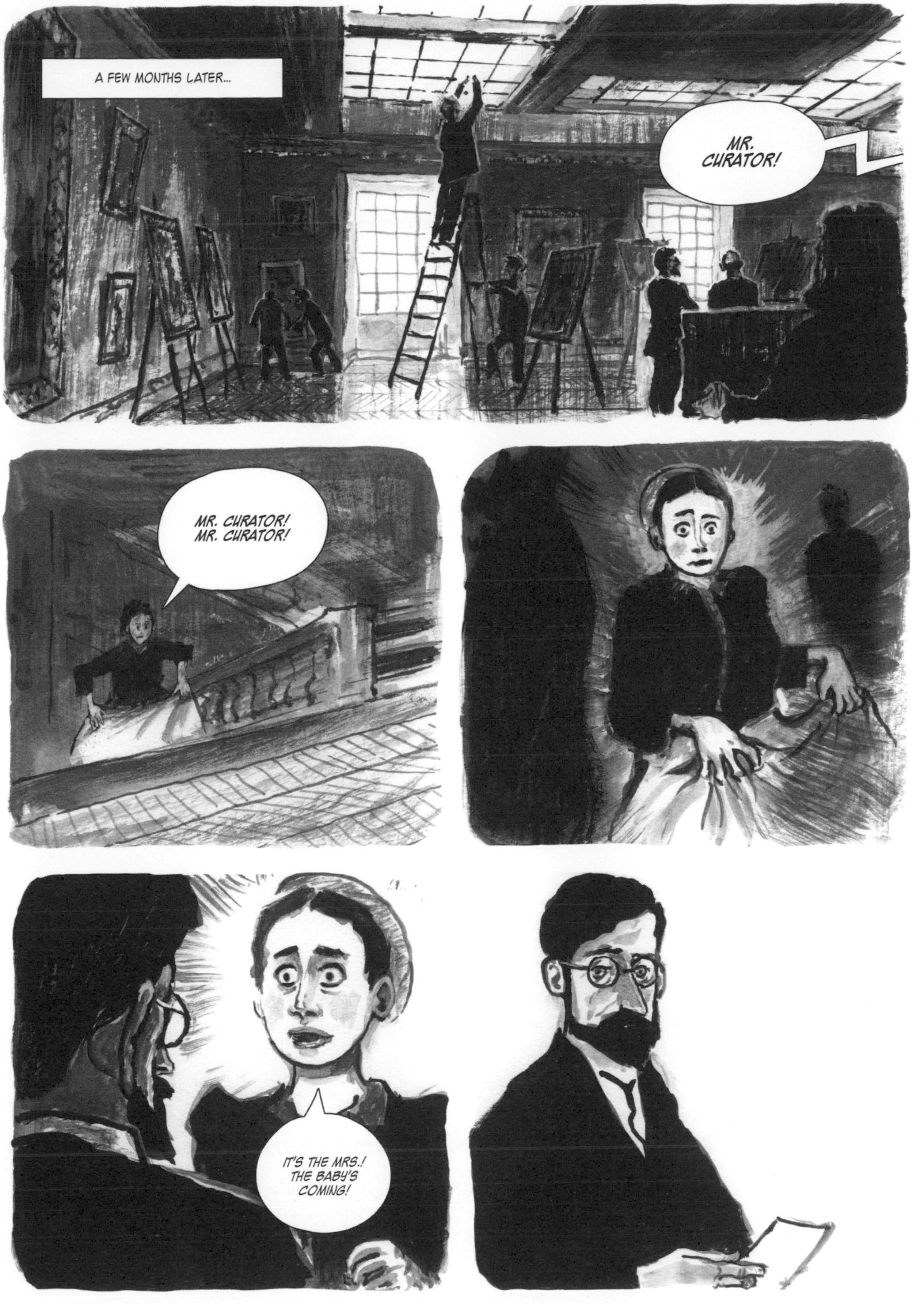
A FEW MONTHS LATER...
MR. CURATOR!
MR. CURATOR! MR. CURATOR!
IT'S THE MRS.! THE BABY'S COMING!

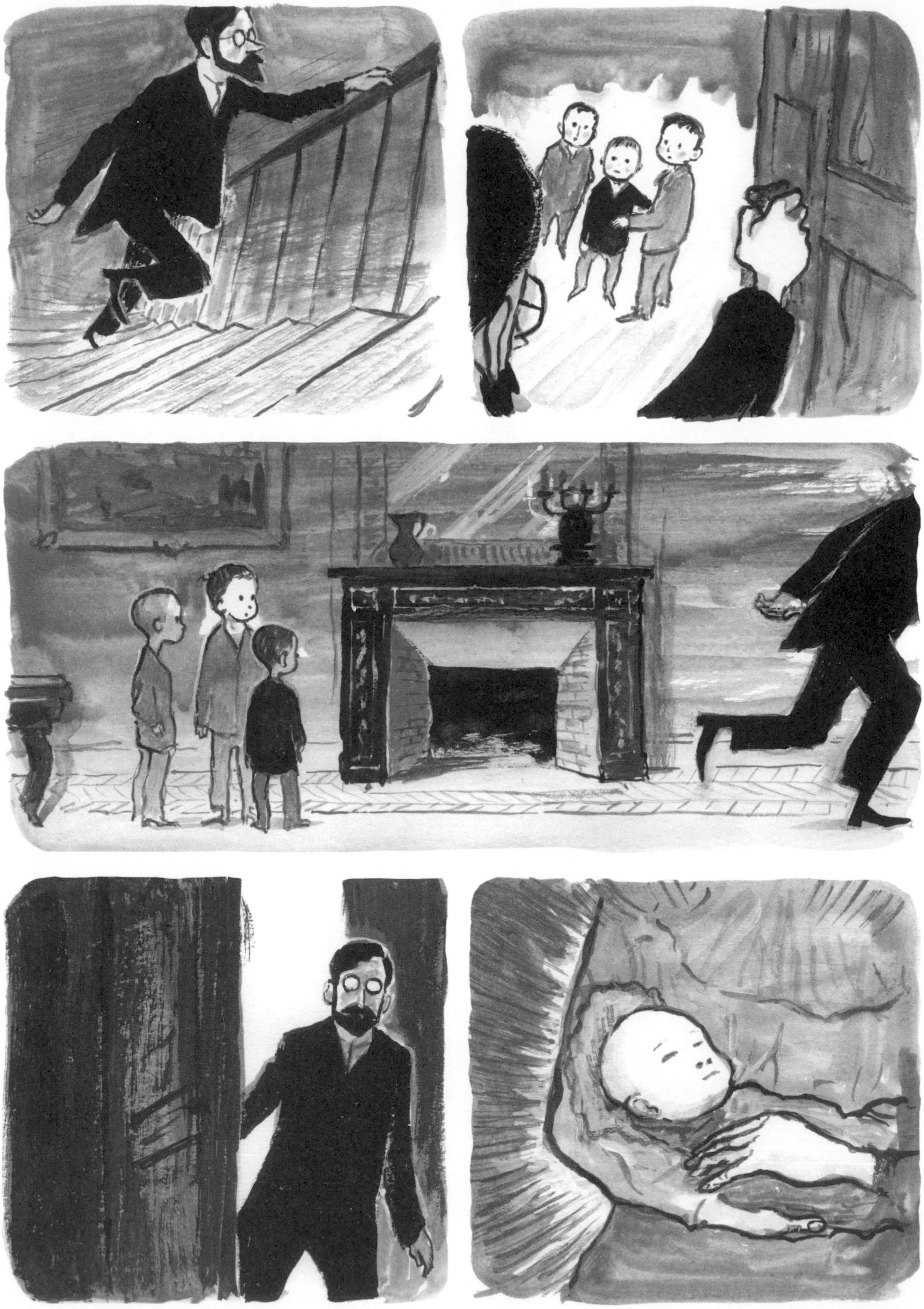

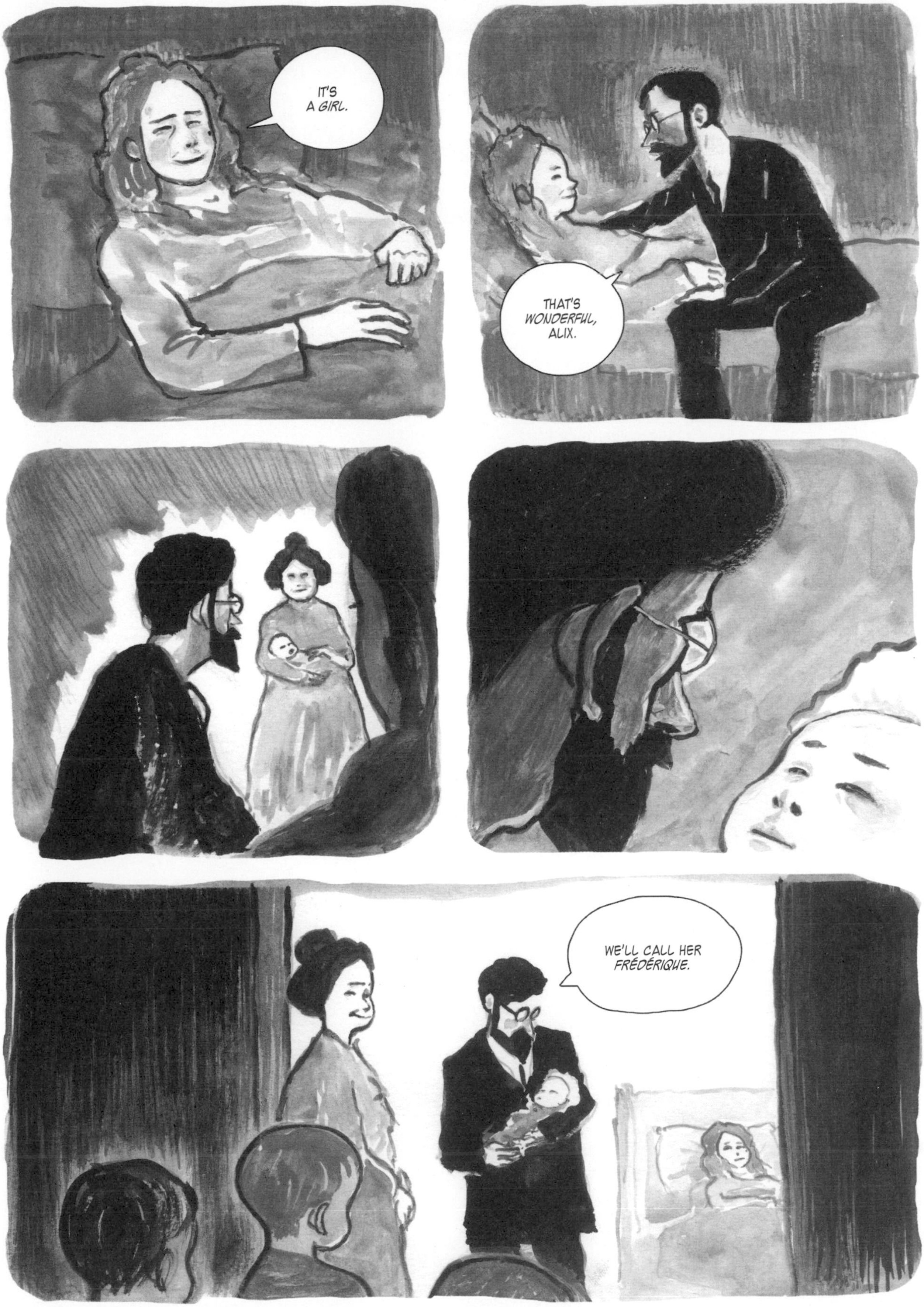
IT'S A GIRL.
THAT'S WONDERFUL, ALIX.
WE'LL CALL HER FRÉDÉRIQUE.

MONDAY, SEPTEMBER 1, 1893, LATE AFTERNOON.

Exhibition
Jean-Marc Nattier
and
the King's D...

ALL THE LATEST FROM VERSAILLES

CURIOSITIES

Some paintings were discovered in Versailles by Mr. Pierre de Nolhac, the palace's curator. These are paintings by Jean-Marc Nattier, a portrait painter for the royal family at the time of Louix XV. An exhibition presenting these findings will be opened this Monday at the Palace of Versailles.

LOOK, PEOPLE ARE COMING!

WE DID RIGHT TO SCHEDULE THE INAUGURATION ON A CLOSING DAY, IT SEEMS TO HAVE AROUSED CURIOSITY.

THIS ARTICLE IN THE LOCAL PRESS IS A BLESSING. IT'S NOT QUITE LE TEMPS, BUT IT'S STILL APPRECIATED.

EXCUSE ME, SIR, I'M TOLD THAT *YOU* ARE RESPONSIBLE FOR ALL THIS, IS THAT SO?

UH... YES, MADAME. PIERRE DE NOLHAC, CHIEF CURATOR AT THE PALACE OF VERSAILLES.

MADAME DE LA VILLIÈRE.

WHAT A *GREAT IDEA* THIS EXHIBITION WAS! IT'S *ABOUT TIME* SOMEONE TOOK CARE OF THIS PALACE. I KNOW HOW LITTLE THE REPUBLIC CARES FOR IT...

THANK YOU, MADAME. BUT MAKE NO MISTAKE, THE REPUBLIC *HAS*, IN FACT, GRANTED US ITS AUTHORIZATION.

THIS INAUGURATION WAS A SMALL-SCALE SUCCESS. SOME PARISIAN CELEBRITIES EVEN MADE THE TRIP. ONE COULD SEE ANATOLE FRANCE, PUVIS DE CHAVANNE, ALPHONSE DAUDET AND AN AMERICAN NAMED JAMES GORDON BENNETT JUNIOR...

IT WAS MENTIONED IN SOME NATIONAL NEWSPAPERS THE FOLLOWING DAY. THE MUSEUM WAS LAUNCHED.

55

FROM THEN ON, THE RESTRUCTURING OF THE ENTIRE MUSEUM WAS STEPPED UP DESPITE LIMITED FINANCIAL RESOURCES. FROM THE GROUND FLOOR TO THE ATTICS, THE COLLECTIONS HAD TO BE SORTED, THE MASTERPIECES DISTINGUISHED FROM THE COPIES, AND THE MUSEUM GALLERIES REFURBISHED.

JACQUOT! MR. DE NOLHAC SAID THIS PAINTING SHOULD GO HERE.

OH, I BEG YOUR PARDON, EUGÈNE DEZILES, SIR.

I FORGOT YOU'RE THE MASTER'S MOUTHPIECE.

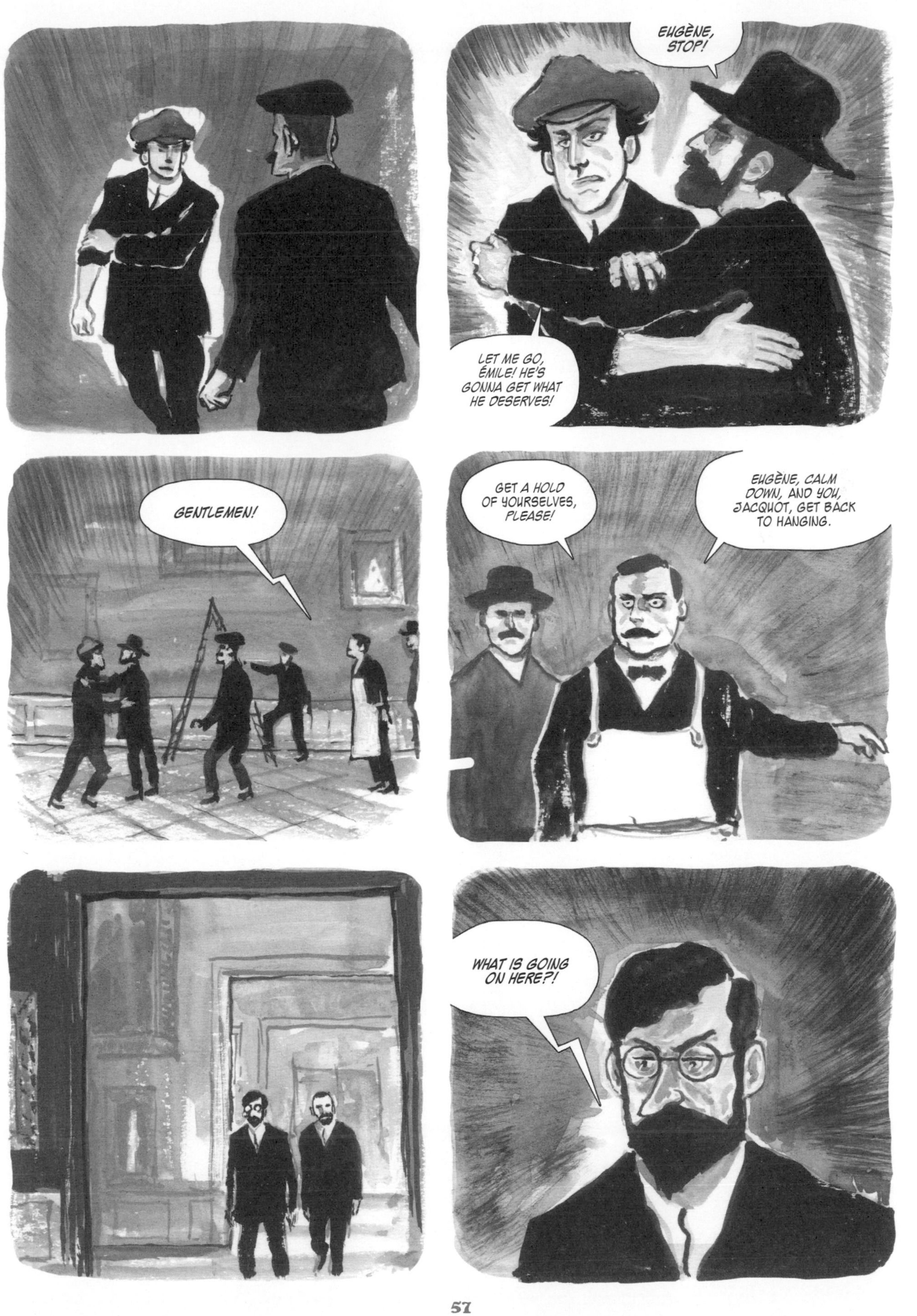
EUGÈNE, STOP!
LET ME GO, ÉMILE! HE'S GONNA GET WHAT HE DESERVES!
GENTLEMEN!
GET A HOLD OF YOURSELVES, PLEASE!
EUGÈNE, CALM DOWN, AND YOU, JACQUOT, GET BACK TO HANGING.
WHAT IS GOING ON HERE?!

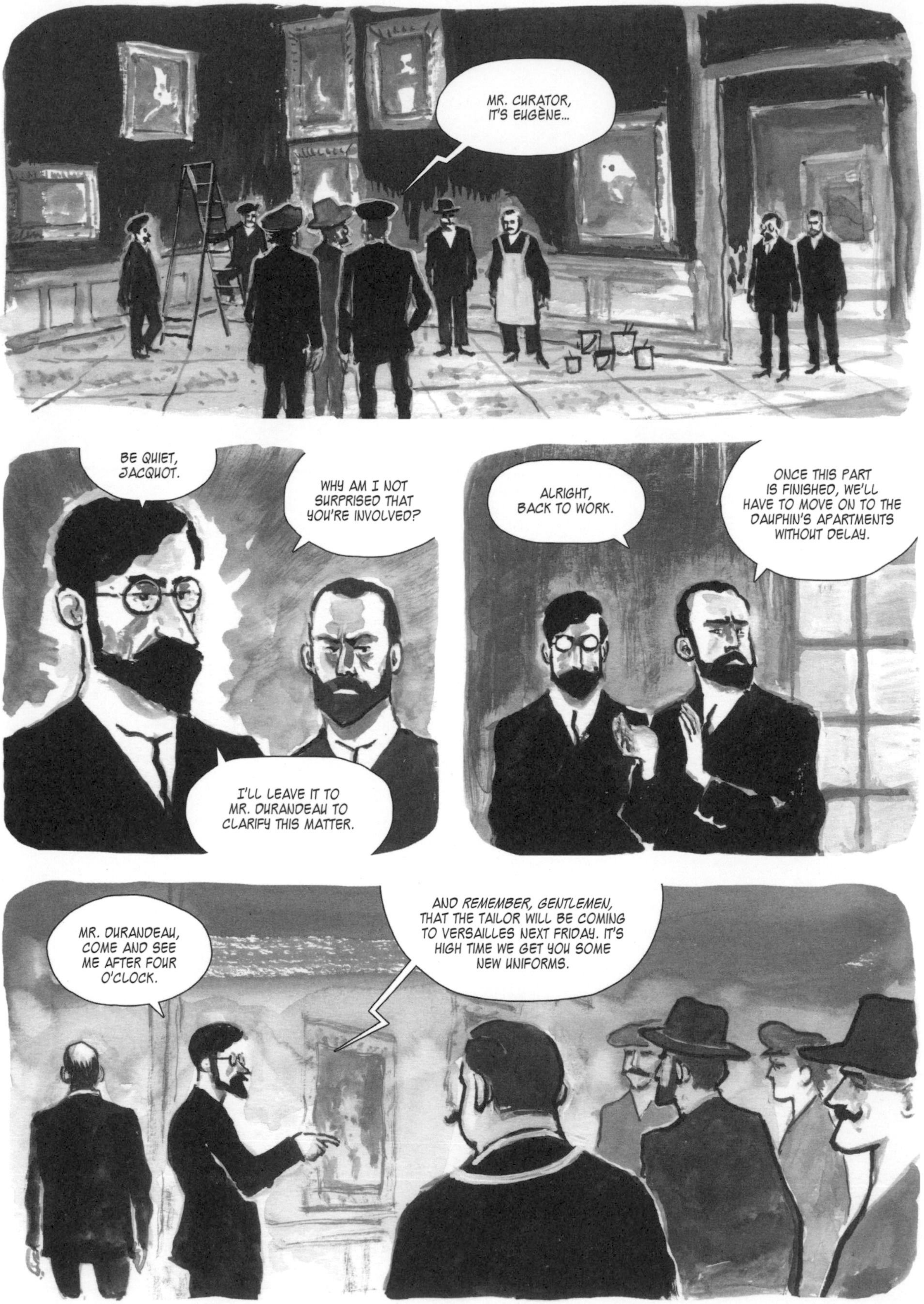
MR. CURATOR, IT'S EUGÈNE...
BE QUIET, JACQUOT.
WHY AM I NOT SURPRISED THAT YOU'RE INVOLVED?
I'LL LEAVE IT TO MR. DURANDEAU TO CLARIFY THIS MATTER.
ALRIGHT, BACK TO WORK.
ONCE THIS PART IS FINISHED, WE'LL HAVE TO MOVE ON TO THE DAUPHIN'S APARTMENTS WITHOUT DELAY.
MR. DURANDEAU, COME AND SEE ME AFTER FOUR O'CLOCK.
AND *REMEMBER*, GENTLEMEN, THAT THE TAILOR WILL BE COMING TO VERSAILLES NEXT FRIDAY. IT'S HIGH TIME WE GET YOU SOME NEW UNIFORMS.

OCTOBER 1896.

EVERYTHING WAS EVENTUALLY SPED INTO MOTION THANKS TO AN UNEXPECTED EVENT...

BAILIFF! HE'S COMING! HAVE SOMEONE NOTIFY ANDRÉ!

GOOD AFTERNOON, GENTLEMEN.

I HAVE VERY LITTLE TIME... TAKE ME TO SEE THE WORK IN PROGRESS RIGHT AWAY.

CERTAINLY, MR. ÉTIENNE. YOU'LL FIND THAT THEY ARE ALREADY *WELL* UNDERWAY. THIS SUDDEN AND RECENT INCREASE IN FUNDING HAS BEEN VERY HELPFUL.

ARE YOU SURE THE BANQUET HALL WILL BE READY IN TIME?

REST ASSURED, THE ENTIRE PALACE IS MOBILIZED FOR THE VISIT.

THIS ROOM WILL BE LIT WITH THE ELECTRICITY THAT THE WORKERS ARE INSTALLING.

HM... CLEARLY, THERE IS STILL WORK TO BE DONE. DON'T FORGET THE *DIPLOMATIC* STAKES OF THIS VISIT.

UNLIKE THE EMPRESS OF PRUSSIA, TSAR NICHOLAS II MUST BE WELCOMED WITH *FULL HONORS* IN ORDER TO STRENGTHEN OUR FRIENDSHIP WITH HIS COUNTRY.

WITHOUT FAIL, MR. ÉTIENNE. THE REPUBLIC'S GOLD WILL SHINE BRIGHTER THAN THE MONARCHY'S LOUIS D'OR.*

*LOUIS D'OR WAS THE GOLD COINAGE INTRODUCED BY LOUIS XIII IN 1640 AND WHICH WAS REPLACED BY THE FRENCH FRANC DURING THE REVOLUTION IN 1795.

OCTOBER 8, 1896.

EVERYTHING WAS READY ON TIME.

THE CROWD GATHERED ON THE SIDEWALKS DISCOVERED THE IMPERIAL COUPLE, ACCOMPANIED BY THE PRESIDENT OF THE FRENCH REPUBLIC, FÉLIX FAURE.

IT WAS NO COINCIDENCE THAT THE MAN KNOWN AS THE "SUN PRESIDENT" HAD CHOSEN VERSAILLES TO WELCOME HIS ALLY.

THE PROCESSION FIRST MADE ITS WAY TO THE GARDENS. THE PALACE STAFF HAD FRONT ROW SEATS FROM BEHIND THE LARGE BAY WINDOWS.

PEOPLE OF FRANCE!

THIRTY THOUSAND FACES THEN TURNED TO FACE THE PALACE. MY FATHER COULD NOT BELIEVE HIS EYES.

*RENE ARMAND FRANCOIS PRUDHOMME, KNOWN AS SULLY PRUDHOMME, A FRENCH POET OF THE SECOND HALF OF THE NINETEENTH CENTURY, RECIPIENT OF THE FIRST NOBEL PRIZE FOR LITERATURE IN 1901.

62

MAY 1898.

WE HAD BEEN LIVING IN THE PALACE FOR TEN YEARS NOW.

MY FATHER HAD US REENACT THE MASTERPIECES OF VERSAILLES TO TEACH US ART HISTORY...

SINCE HE WAS THE OLDEST, PAOLO WAS LOUIS XIV, I WAS MARS, THE GOD OF WAR, MARIE-LOUISE WAS MINERVA, GODDESS OF MANY TALENTS, FRANÇOIS WAS A YOUNG SOLDIER, AND FRÉDÉRIQUE WAS A LITTLE ANGEL WITH HER PLAYING CARDS IN HER HANDS.

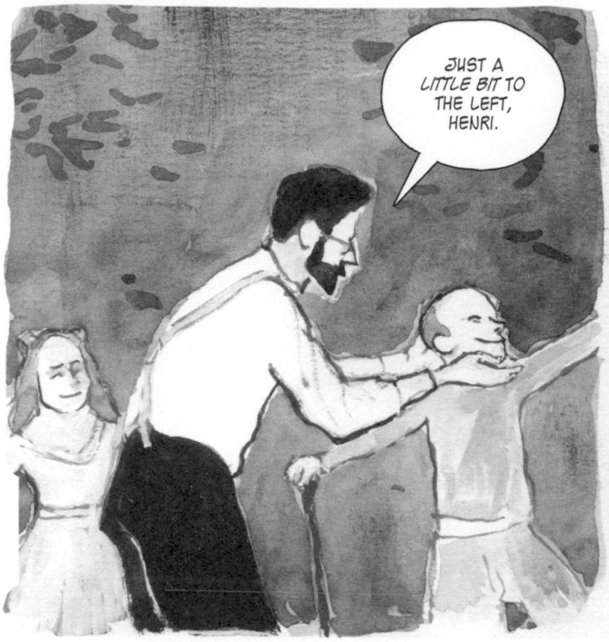
JUST A LITTLE BIT TO THE LEFT, HENRI.

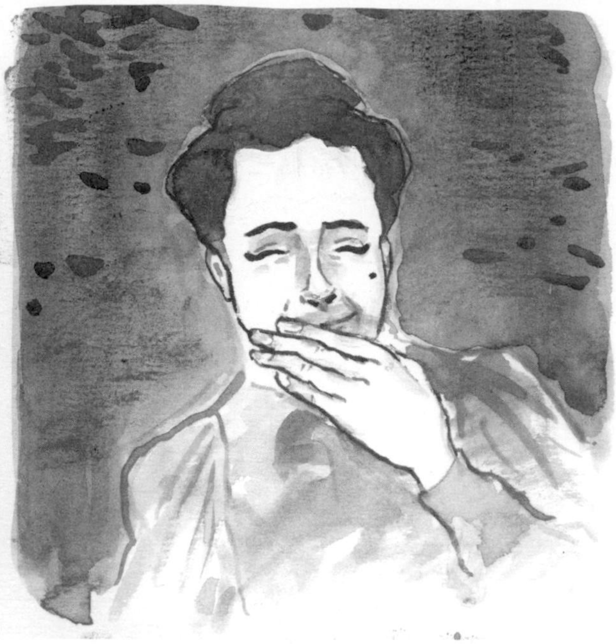

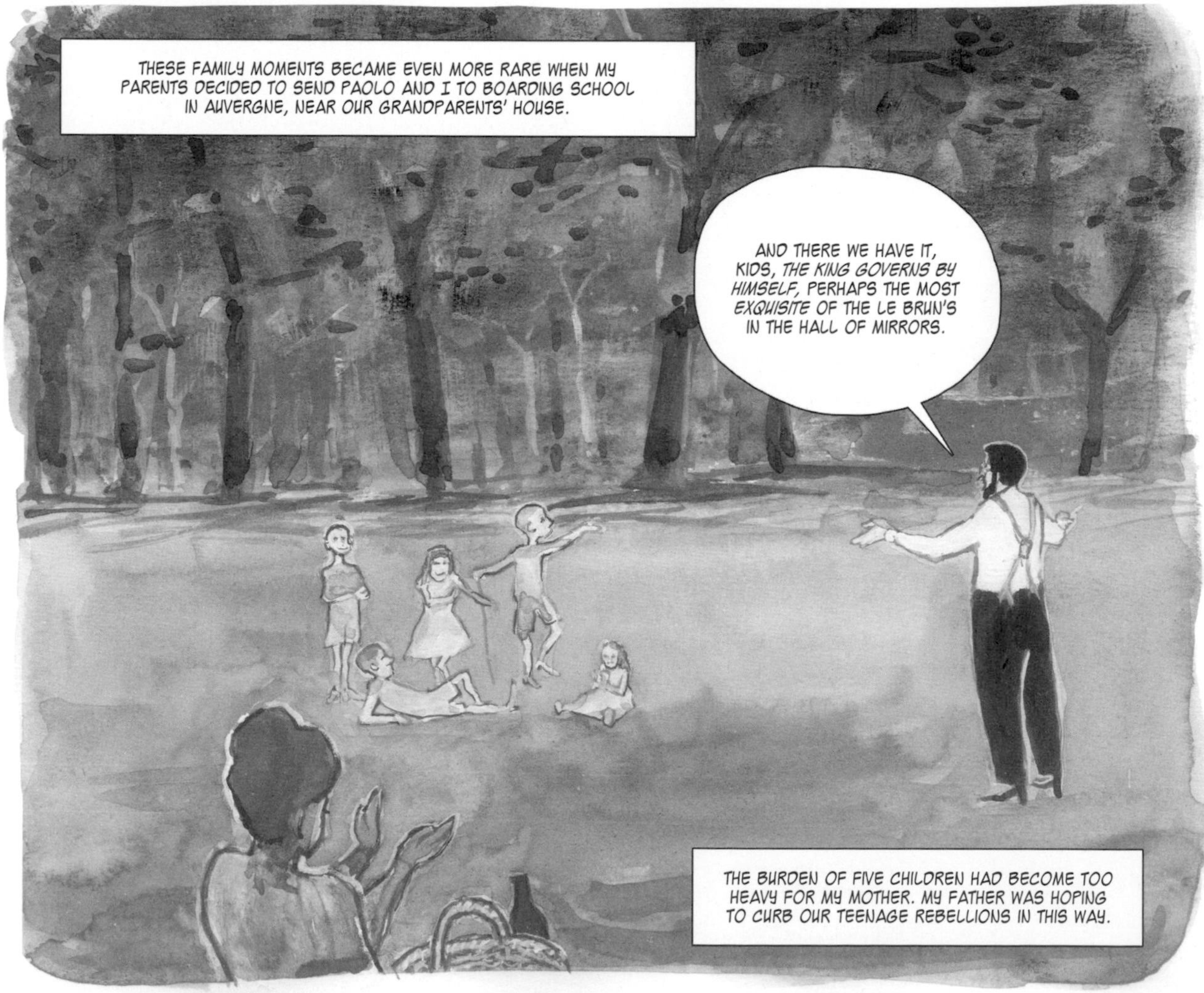
THESE FAMILY MOMENTS BECAME EVEN MORE RARE WHEN MY PARENTS DECIDED TO SEND PAOLO AND I TO BOARDING SCHOOL IN AUVERGNE, NEAR OUR GRANDPARENTS' HOUSE.
AND THERE WE HAVE IT, KIDS, THE KING GOVERNS BY HIMSELF, PERHAPS THE MOST EXQUISITE OF THE LE BRUN'S IN THE HALL OF MIRRORS.
THE BURDEN OF FIVE CHILDREN HAD BECOME TOO HEAVY FOR MY MOTHER. MY FATHER WAS HOPING TO CURB OUR TEENAGE REBELLIONS IN THIS WAY.

SUNDAY, MAY 19, 1935.

IT'S ME!

SO HOW'S YOUR FATHER DOING?

A BIT BETTER.

BUT I'M WORRIED ABOUT HIS HEALTH, AND HE WON'T LISTEN TO ANY ADVICE.

AH, WELL, HE'S SET IN HIS WAYS!
ARE THE GIRLS HERE?
NO, THEY WENT TO THE CINEMA WITH THE NEIGHBOR'S HOUSEKEEPER.
THEY WERE DYING TO SEE GARY COOPER!
I HAVE TO CALL MARIE-LOUISE, I PROMISED TO GIVE HER SOME NEWS ABOUT FATHER.
YOU SHOULD ALSO CALL YOUR MOTHER...
I KNOW...

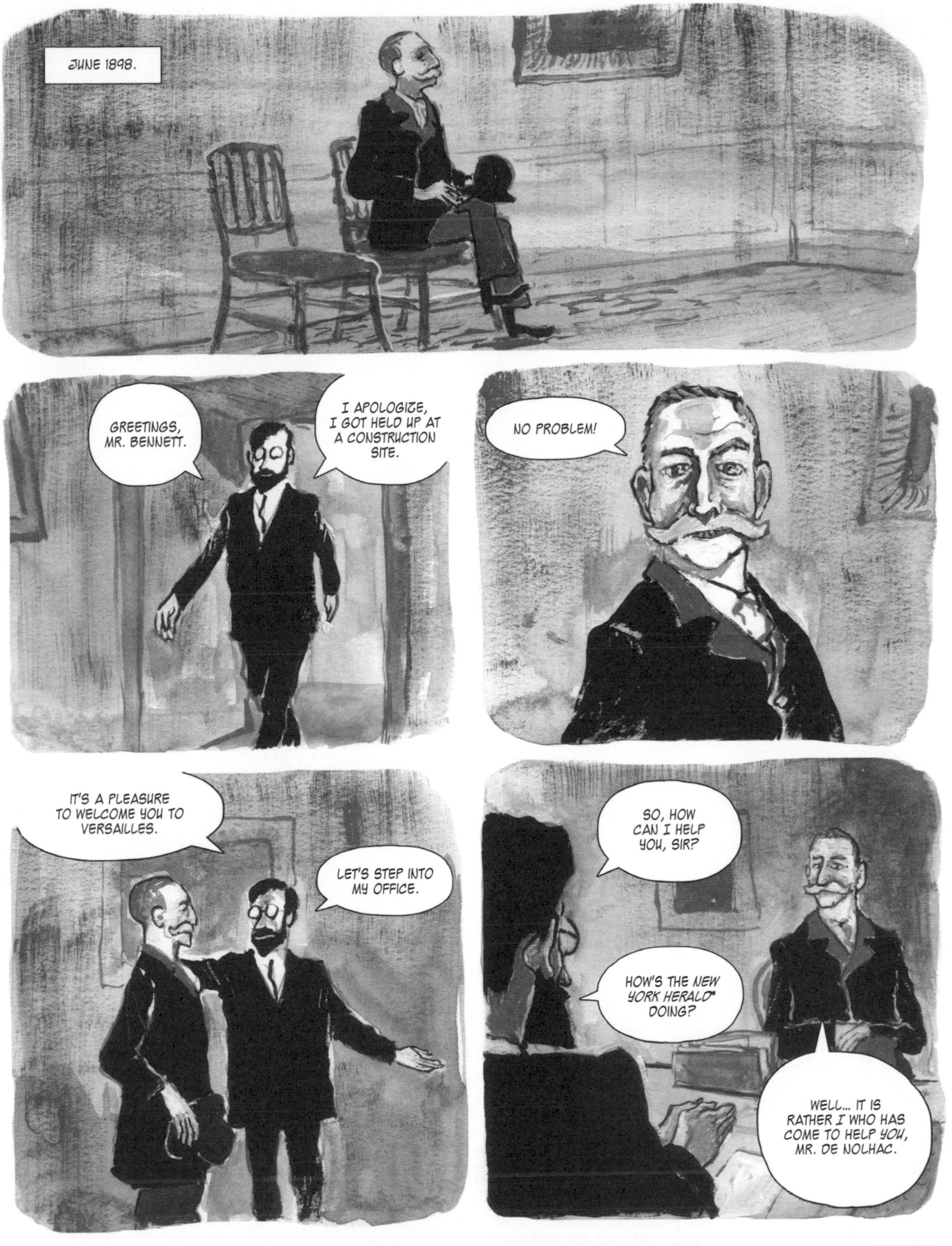
JUNE 1898.
GREETINGS, MR. BENNETT.
I APOLOGIZE, I GOT HELD UP AT A CONSTRUCTION SITE.
NO PROBLEM!
IT'S A PLEASURE TO WELCOME YOU TO VERSAILLES.
LET'S STEP INTO MY OFFICE.
SO, HOW CAN I HELP YOU, SIR?
HOW'S THE *NEW YORK HERALD** DOING?
WELL… IT IS RATHER *I* WHO HAS COME TO HELP *YOU*, MR. DE NOLHAC.

*ON OCTOBER 4, 1887, IN PARIS, JAMES GORDON BENNETT LAUNCHED THE EUROPEAN EDITION OF THE FAMOUS *NEW YORK HERALD*, AN AMERICAN NEWSPAPER WITH A LARGE CIRCULATION CREATED BY HIS FATHER IN 1835. AS HIS BUY-OUTS PROGRESSED, THE EUROPEAN EDITION WAS RENAMED *INTERNATIONAL HERALD TRIBUNE* IN 1966 AND, RECENTLY, *INTERNATIONAL NEW YORK TIMES*. IN 2016, THE NEWSPAPER ULTIMATELY LEFT PARIS.

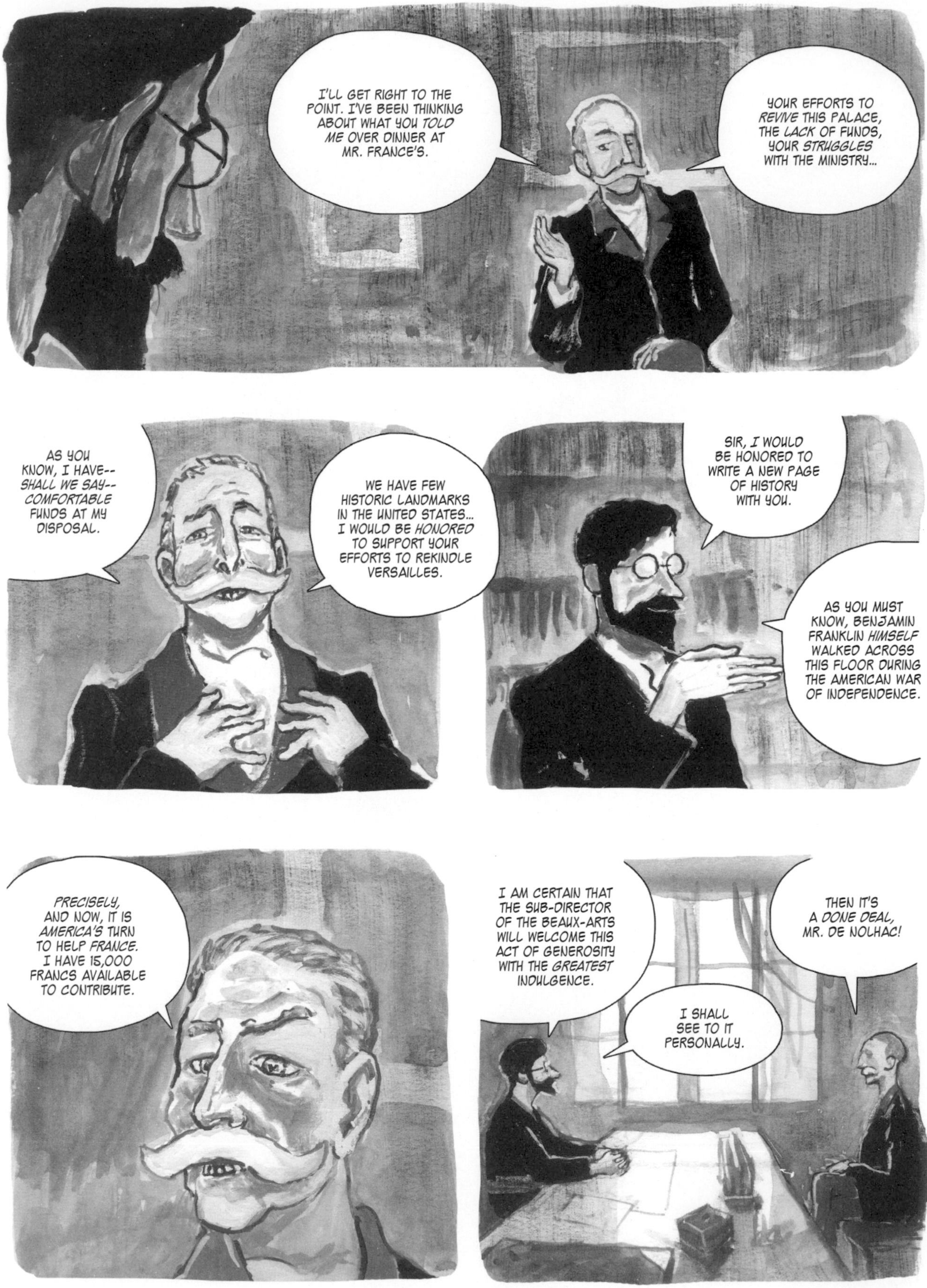
I'LL GET RIGHT TO THE POINT. I'VE BEEN THINKING ABOUT WHAT YOU *TOLD ME* OVER DINNER AT MR. FRANCE'S.
YOUR EFFORTS TO *REVIVE* THIS PALACE, THE *LACK* OF FUNDS, YOUR *STRUGGLES* WITH THE MINISTRY...
AS YOU KNOW, I HAVE-- *SHALL WE SAY-- COMFORTABLE* FUNDS AT MY DISPOSAL.
WE HAVE FEW HISTORIC LANDMARKS IN THE UNITED STATES... I WOULD BE *HONORED* TO SUPPORT YOUR EFFORTS TO REKINDLE VERSAILLES.
SIR, *I* WOULD BE HONORED TO WRITE A NEW PAGE OF HISTORY WITH YOU.
AS YOU MUST KNOW, BENJAMIN FRANKLIN *HIMSELF* WALKED ACROSS THIS FLOOR DURING THE AMERICAN WAR OF INDEPENDENCE.
PRECISELY, AND NOW, IT IS *AMERICA'S* TURN TO HELP *FRANCE.* I HAVE 15,000 FRANCS AVAILABLE TO CONTRIBUTE.
I AM CERTAIN THAT THE SUB-DIRECTOR OF THE BEAUX-ARTS WILL WELCOME THIS ACT OF GENEROSITY WITH THE *GREATEST* INDULGENCE.
THEN IT'S A *DONE DEAL,* MR. DE NOLHAC!
I SHALL SEE TO IT PERSONALLY.

YOU TOLD ME THE OTHER DAY THAT THERE ARE NEARLY 1,500 FEATURES OF VERSAILLES IN NEED OF TENDING. WHICH ONES ARE YOU WORKING ON AT THE MOMENT?

AS I WAS SAYING, THE COLLECTIONS MUST BE REORGANIZED IN SEVERAL--

AH, MR. DE NOLHAC!

YES? TO WHOM DO I OWE THE HONOR...?

HELLO, ALLOW ME TO INTRODUCE MYSELF: MR. DE VAL, RETIRED BATTALION COMMANDER AND NEW PRESIDENT OF THE DEFENSE COMMITTEE FOR THE CONSERVATION OF THE CITY, THE PALACE, AND THE ESTATE OF VERSAILLES.

WELL THEN, MR. DE VAL, WHAT CAN I DO FOR YOU?

THE COMMITTEE AND I WOULD LIKE THE KING'S HALL TO BE *RELOCATED* TO THE GROUND FLOOR.

WE FIND IT *DISHONORABLE* TO THE MEMORY OF OUR MONARCHS THAT THIS ROOM HAS BEEN OUTRIGHT *DISMANTLED!*

I HEAR YOUR CONCERN, SIR.

PLEASE INFORM THE COMMITTEE THAT THE KINGS OF FRANCE HAVE NEVER ACTUALLY *SEEN* THIS ROOM, SINCE IT'S DECOR WAS *INVENTED* BY LOUIS-PHILIPPE.

BUT PERHAPS I COULD INVITE THE COMMITTEE FOR A VISIT?

THEY WILL BE ABLE TO SEE FOR THEMSELVES THAT WE HAVE GIVEN PRIDE OF PLACE TO THE KINGS OF FRANCE BY REARRANGING THE COLLECTIONS.

AHEM--YES, THAT SOUNDS GOOD. SEND YOUR INVITATION TO FOUR, RUE HOCHE.

BUT DON'T THINK WE'LL BE *COAXED* INTO ANYTHING, WE WILL *ALWAYS* LOOK AFTER VERSAILLES.

AS YOU MAY HAVE NOTICED, SOME VERSAILLES RESIDENTS AREN'T TOO OPEN TO CHANGE. THEY GO SO FAR AS TO COLLECT THE COMPLAINTS FROM CUSTODIANS WHO ARE CONCERNED THAT THEIR WORKLOAD WILL INCREASE NOW THAT WE HAVE RE-OPENED THE MUSEUM.

LET'S GO SEE THE UPCOMING RENOVATION OF THE EIGHTEENTH CENTURY ROOMS. THEY'RE AT THE HEART OF THE PALACE.

THIS IS WHAT YOUR GENEROUS DONATION COULD BE USED FOR, MR. BENNETT! TO RESTORE THESE PLACES TO THEIR ORIGINAL GLORY.

THAT'S FANTASTIC, MR. DE NOLHAC...

PARIS, THE LOUVRE MUSEUM. JUNE 1898.

HELLO, PIERRE.

MR. LAFENESTRE, THANK YOU FOR SEEING ME FOR THIS--SHALL WE SAY--EXCEPTIONAL REQUEST.

OR AT LEAST, "UNPRECEDENTED"! PLEASE, CALL ME GEORGES, WE'RE COLLEAGUES, AFTER ALL.

I CAN'T HELP BUT IMAGINE WHAT THIS SQUARE LOOKED LIKE BEFORE THE PARIS COMMUNE, WHEN THE TUILERIES PALACE HAD A FOURTH WING.

YES, IT IS FAIR TO SAY THAT THE COMMUNARDS DID NOT GO ABOUT THEIR BUSINESS HALF-HEARTEDLY.

WHAT CAN YOU DO, THERE WEREN'T ENOUGH FUNDS AND THE GOVERNMENT HAD RATHER REBUILD THE TOWN HALL THAN THE TUILERIES PALACE.

THIS MAZE OF CORRIDORS REMINDS ME OF VERSAILLES.

I'M SURE IT DOES.

YOU COULD TAKE THIS *WHOLE LOT*, FOR EXAMPLE! THEY'RE NOT IN TOO TERRIBLE A CONDITION.

THIS IS EXACTLY WHAT WE NEED.

I'LL BE SURE TO ANNOTATE ALL THE FRAMES THAT COME FROM THE LOUVRE.

DON'T WORRY ABOUT IT, PIERRE.

GENTLEMEN, TAKE THIS DOWN TO THE COURTYARD, THESE ARE TO BE LOADED ON THE CART FOR VERSAILLES.

A PISTON-ENGINE-POWERED AUTOMOBILE SHOW WILL SOON BE HOSTED AT THE TUILERIES.

IN FACT, THE MINISTRY INTENDS TO EXPLORE THE POSSIBILITIES OF MOTORIZING THE GOVERNMENT'S VEHICLES.

THAT MAY BE A LITTLE HASTY--I READ SOMEWHERE THAT AUTOMOBILE MECHANICS ARE NOT VERY RELIABLE...

I DON'T KNOW HOW TO THANK YOU, GEORGES.

OUR FINANCES ARE AT THEIR LOWEST. BUT THANKS TO YOU, WE ARE MAKING SIGNIFICANT SAVINGS.

YOU'RE WELCOME, PIERRE. BUT DON'T MENTION ANYTHING ABOUT OUR ARRANGEMENTS TO THE MINISTRY, I DON'T THINK THEY'D APPRECIATE IT...

AND AVOID RUE DE RIVOLI, THE STREET IS CLOSED DUE TO THE CONSTRUCTION OF THE METROPOLITAN.

JUNE 12, 1898.

I'LL TRY MY LUCK AT THE CHAT NOIR... LA, LA, LA...

DOWN AT YOUR CABARET, I ORDER A DOUBLE, I BEAT IN YOUR FACE, AND WIPE OFF MY KNUCKLES!

MARIE-LOUISE!

WHAT'S THE MATTER, MAMA?

WHAT ARE YOU SINGING?!

I TAUGHT HER MOTHER, IT'S THE MONTMARTRE SONG!

I KNOW, FRANÇOIS. BUT WHERE DID YOU GET ALL THIS CABARET POPPYCOCK?

FROM DÉDÉ, MR. ÉMILE'S SON.

75

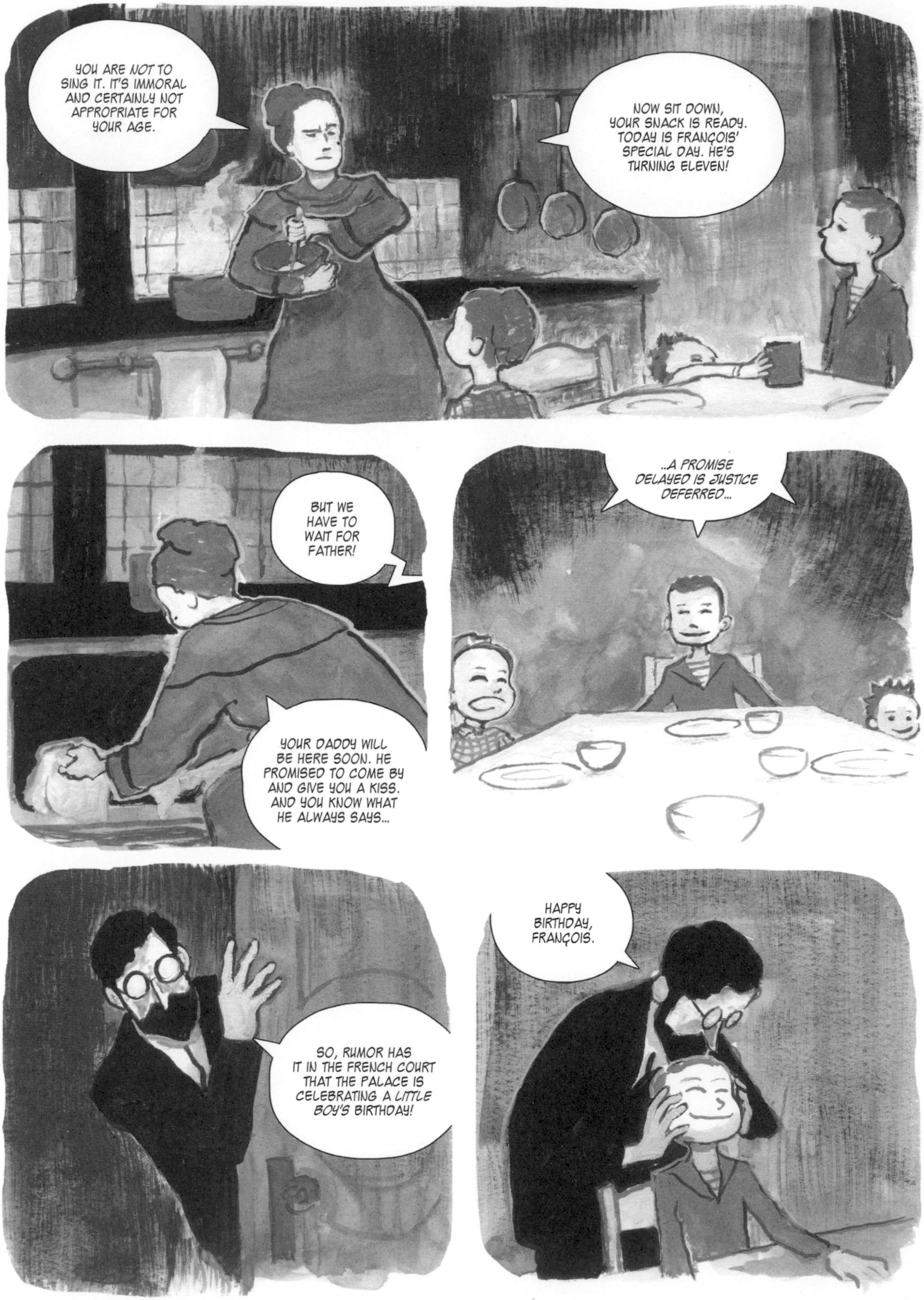
YOU ARE *NOT* TO SING IT. IT'S IMMORAL AND CERTAINLY NOT APPROPRIATE FOR YOUR AGE.
NOW SIT DOWN, YOUR SNACK IS READY. TODAY IS FRANÇOIS' SPECIAL DAY. HE'S TURNING ELEVEN!
BUT WE HAVE TO WAIT FOR FATHER!
YOUR DADDY WILL BE HERE SOON. HE PROMISED TO COME BY AND GIVE YOU A KISS. AND YOU KNOW WHAT HE ALWAYS SAYS...
...A PROMISE DELAYED IS JUSTICE DEFERRED...
SO, RUMOR HAS IT IN THE FRENCH COURT THAT THE PALACE IS CELEBRATING A *LITTLE* BOY'S BIRTHDAY!
HAPPY BIRTHDAY, FRANÇOIS.

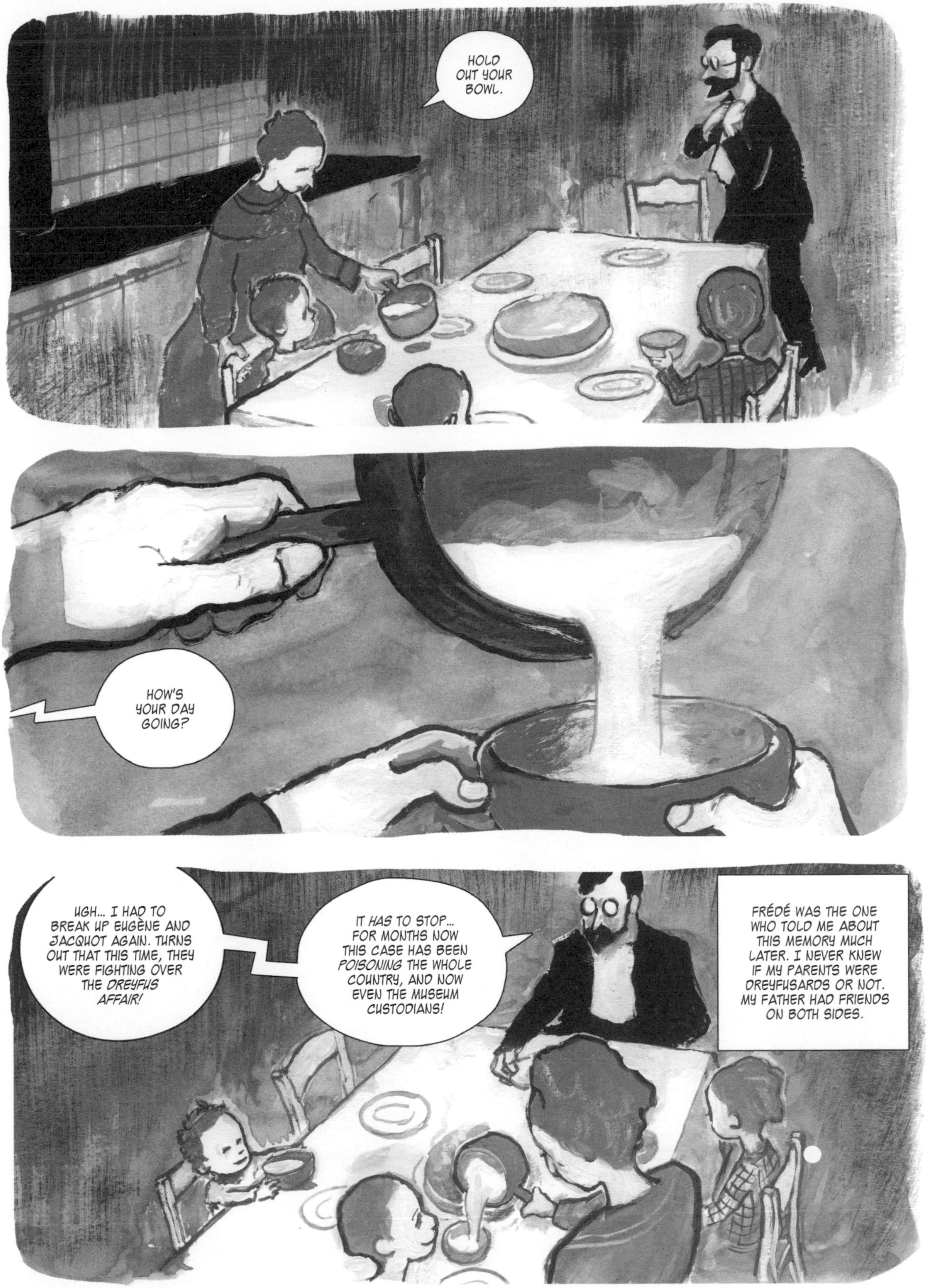
HOLD OUT YOUR BOWL.
HOW'S YOUR DAY GOING?
UGH... I HAD TO BREAK UP EUGÈNE AND JACQUOT AGAIN. TURNS OUT THAT THIS TIME, THEY WERE FIGHTING OVER THE *DREYFUS AFFAIR!*
IT *HAS* TO STOP... FOR MONTHS NOW THIS CASE HAS BEEN *POISONING* THE WHOLE COUNTRY, AND NOW EVEN THE MUSEUM CUSTODIANS!
FRÉDÉ WAS THE ONE WHO TOLD ME ABOUT THIS MEMORY MUCH LATER. I NEVER KNEW IF MY PARENTS WERE DREYFUSARDS OR NOT. MY FATHER HAD FRIENDS ON BOTH SIDES.

JULY 1898, ONE MONTH LATER.

PIERRE!

MARIE-LOUISE...

OH, MY DEAR BROTHER!

THANK YOU FOR COMING ON SUCH SHORT NOTICE.

I DON'T KNOW WHAT'S WRONG, IT'S BEEN SO BRUTAL.

IS HE NOT GETTING ANY BETTER?

HE'S BEEN GETTING WEAKER SINCE THE OPERATION... HE'S AT THE GRAND COMMUN MILITARY HOSPITAL.

I WAS ABLE TO GET AN EXCEPTIONAL AUTHORIZATION.

HE'LL BE HAPPY TO SEE HIS AUNT, I'M SURE!

ALIX...

I'LL TAKE THE KIDS FOR A WALK IN THE PARK. GO HOME AND GET SOME REST.

COME, ALIX, THERE'S NOTHING MORE WE CAN DO.

NO! YOU GO HOME IF YOU WANT, BACK TO THAT *WRETCHED* PALACE!

I *REFUSE* TO LEAVE MY BABY ALONE!

MY BROTHER FRANÇOIS DIED THE NEXT DAY, ON JULY 10, 1898. THIS TRAGEDY
WOULD REMAIN UNEXPLAINED, WHICH MADE IT ALL THE MORE CRUEL. PAOLO AND
I CAME HOME IN A PANIC FROM OUR BOARDING SCHOOL IN CLERMONT. THE WAKE
LASTED UNTIL THE EARLY MORNING. I SPENT THE NIGHT DRAWING THE ROOM. EVEN
AFTER HIS DEATH, I THINK FRANÇOIS HAS ALWAYS BEEN MY FATHER'S FAVORITE.

NOVEMBER 1898.

WHAT ARE YOU DOING?!

I'M DISMANTLING THE FACADE'S SCULPTURES.

HAVE YOU NOT READ MY REPORT ON THEIR STATE OF DEGRADATION?

YES, OF COURSE. BUT WHY, IN GOD'S NAME, SAW THEM OFF?

IT MAKES IT EASIER FOR MY MEN TO TAKE THEM DOWN.

AT THAT TIME, THE ARCHITECTS OF HISTORIC MONUMENTS HAD FULL POWER OVER THE PALACE'S STRUCTURE. CONSERVATION WORK WAS STRICTLY LIMITED TO THE COLLECTIONS. MARCEL LAMBERT SEIZED THE OPPORTUNITY TO CARRY OUT THE RESTORATIONS AS HE WISHED, WITHOUT ANY KIND OF CONSULTATION.

MARCEL! I STRONGLY OBJECT!

THIS IS PURE VANDALISM!

WE'VE BEEN OVER THIS *TIME* AND *TIME* AGAIN...

YOU'VE ALREADY *DISREGARDED* THE SOURCES AND RESTORED THE ROOF OF THE DAUPHIN'S LIBRARY WITH *VERY QUESTIONABLE* TASTE!

COME ON, PIERRE, DON'T MAKE SUCH A BIG DEAL: SOON, BRAND NEW COPIES WILL REPLACE THEM.

YOU WON'T BE ABLE TO TELL THE DIFFERENCE!

YEAH, RIGHT... THIS SO-CALLED "RENOVATION" IS NOTHING BUT A MASSACRE!

FOR GOD'S SAKE, HAVE YOU EVEN *READ* THE ARCHITECTURAL HANDBOOK IN OUR ARCHIVES?!

YOU KEEP BUGGING ME WITH YOUR *OLD BOOKS*, DE NOLHAC.

PIERRE, WHAT'S GOING ON?!

MARCEL IS UNSCRUPULOUSLY *DESTROYING* THE LEGACY OF AN ENTIRE NATION...

WELL, WELL... YOU'VE NEVER ACCUSED ME OF HIGH TREASON BEFORE.

I ACCUSE YOU OF DOING AS *YOU PLEASE*...

STUDY THE SOURCES, *REVIEW* THE ORIGINAL DRAWINGS AND *UNDERSTAND* OUR PREDECESSORS. *RESPECT THEIR GENIUS!*

I WON'T LET THIS SLIDE, MARCEL, I'M WRITING A LETTER TO THE BEAUX-ARTS.

COME ON NOW, PIERRE! YOU WON'T HAVE ME BELIEVE THAT THESE ARE *MASTERPIECES.* IF THAT'S THE CASE, THEN WHY DID THEY PLACE THEM HERE, OUT OF SIGHT?

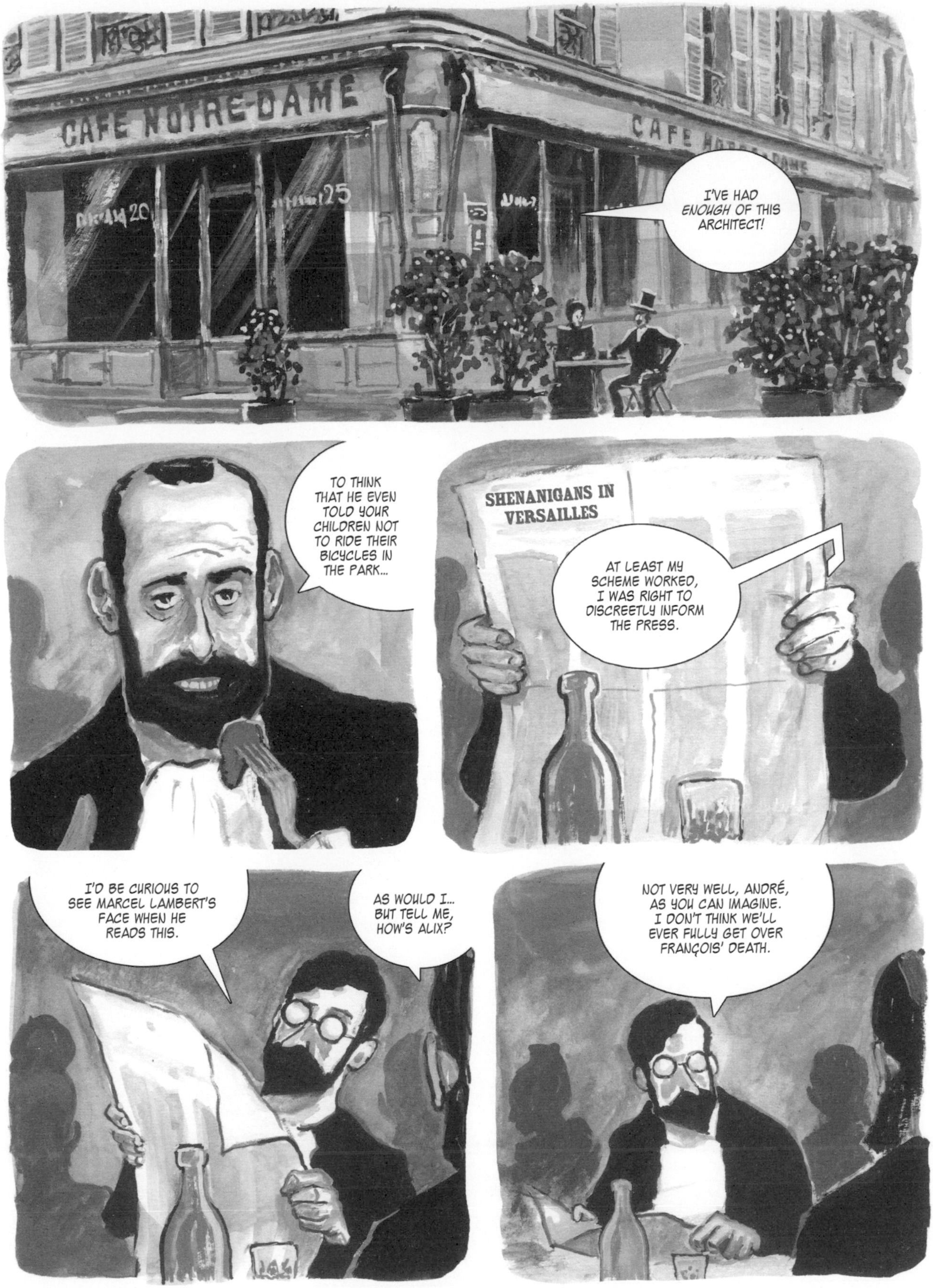
CAFE NOTRE-DAME
I'VE HAD *ENOUGH* OF THIS ARCHITECT!
TO THINK THAT HE EVEN TOLD YOUR CHILDREN NOT TO RIDE THEIR BICYCLES IN THE PARK...
SHENANIGANS IN VERSAILLES
AT LEAST MY SCHEME WORKED, I WAS RIGHT TO DISCREETLY INFORM THE PRESS.
I'D BE CURIOUS TO SEE MARCEL LAMBERT'S FACE WHEN HE READS THIS.
AS WOULD I... BUT TELL ME, HOW'S ALIX?
NOT VERY WELL, ANDRÉ, AS YOU CAN IMAGINE. I DON'T THINK WE'LL EVER FULLY GET OVER FRANÇOIS' DEATH.

DECEMBER 31, 1899.

HURRY UP, IT'S ALMOST MIDNIGHT!

YES, WE'RE COMING! WE'RE RIGHT BEHIND YOU!

JUST A FEW MORE MINUTES...

ALRIGHT, PASSEMANT. LET'S SEE IF YOUR ASTRONOMICAL CLOCK MAKES IT INTO THE NEW CENTURY.

IT IS JANUARY THE FIRST, 1900! HAPPY NEW YEAR TO YOU ALL!

Chapter 3
VERSAILLES, THE NEW TREND

PARIS. APRIL 14, 1900.

I ALWAYS BELIEVED THAT THE TWENTIETH CENTURY HAD BEGUN ON THAT SPRING DAY, WITH THE INAUGURATION OF THE EXPOSITION UNIVERSELLE.

MODERNITY TRIUMPHED IN PARIS, BEFORE THE ENTIRE WORLD: MR. DIESEL'S ENGINES, THE GRANDE ROUE DE PARIS...

THE LUMIÈRE BROTHERS' CINEMATOGRAPH, THE MOVING SIDEWALK, NAMED "RUE DE L'AVENIR"*...

*"STREET OF THE FUTURE."

OF COURSE, VERSAILLES PLAYED ITS PART. MY FATHER HAD GRANTED EXCEPTIONAL LOANS FOR THE ART EXHIBITION AT THE BRAND NEW GRAND PALAIS.

WELL, DE NOLHAC, I SEE THAT *ALL* OF VERSAILLES IS HERE!

THAT'S RIGHT, PHILIPPE, NOBODY WANTED TO MISS THIS EVENT.

WELL, LOOK AT THAT!

NEITHER DID *LE FIGARO'S* ENTIRE EDITORIAL TEAM.

AND IT'S A PERFECT DAY TO ENJOY THE "GOOD AIR" OF PARIS.

IT'S, ABOVE ALL, A GREAT OPPORTUNITY TO PRESENT OUR MASTERPIECES TO THE REST OF THE WORLD.

I AM JUST *DELIGHTED* THAT THE LOUVRE IS ASSOCIATED WITH THIS.

GENTLEMEN OF THE LOUVRE, BEWARE: VERSAILLES HAS BECOME A SERIOUS COMPETITOR TO YOUR INSTITUTION!

AH! I HAVE A FEELING THIS NEW CENTURY WILL HAVE MANY SURPRISES IN STORE FOR US!

MOTHER...

89

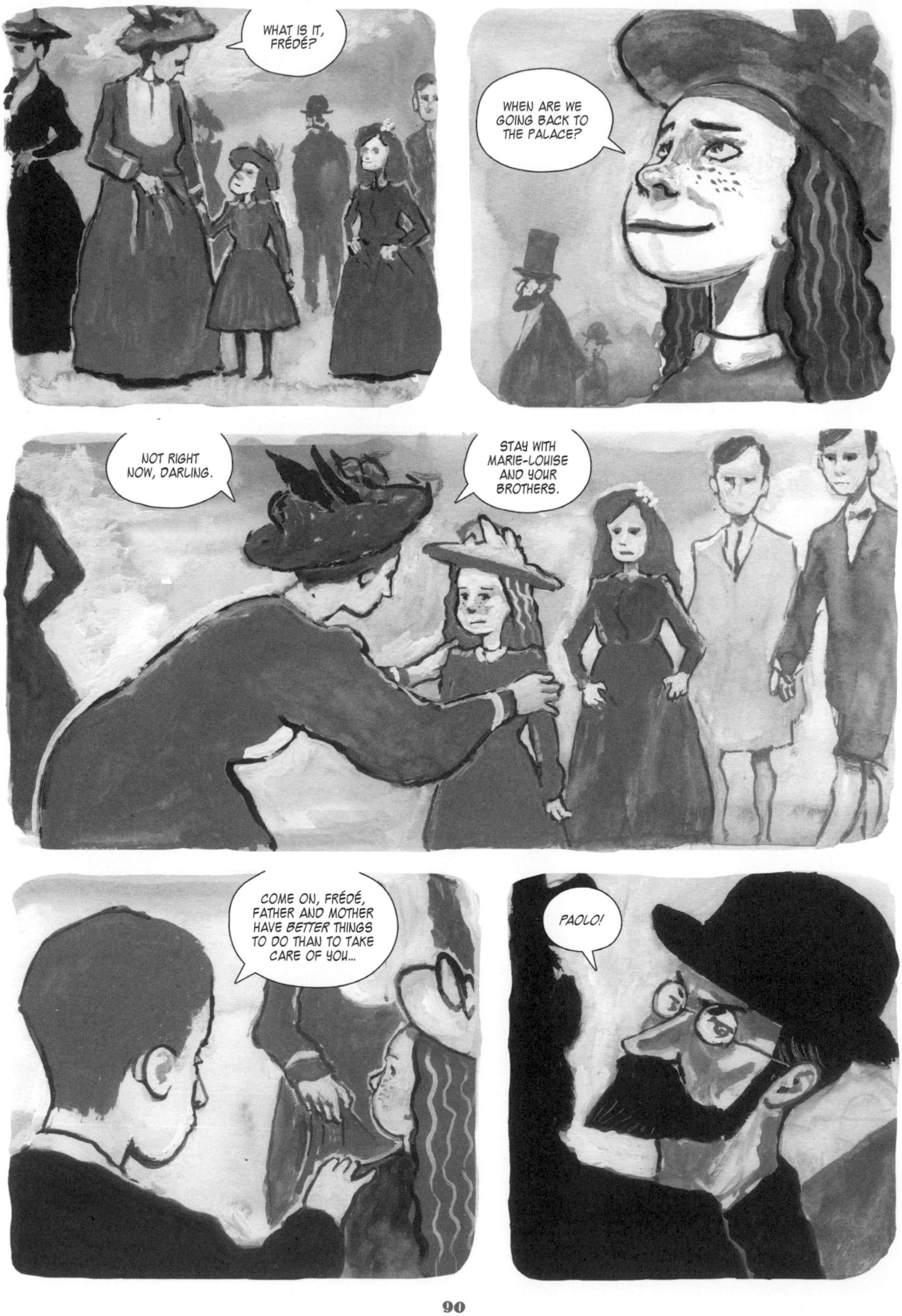
WHAT IS IT, FRÉDÉ?
WHEN ARE WE GOING BACK TO THE PALACE?
NOT RIGHT NOW, DARLING.
STAY WITH MARIE-LOUISE AND YOUR BROTHERS.
COME ON, FRÉDÉ, FATHER AND MOTHER HAVE *BETTER* THINGS TO DO THAN TO TAKE CARE OF YOU...
PAOLO!

THE NEXT DAY.

WHAM!

PAO!

PAOLO! WAIT!

FORGET IT, HENRI! FATHER WILL NEVER CHANGE! BESIDES, HE'S ONLY INTERESTED IN VERSAILLES.

IT'S NOT THAT BAD, PAOLO.

HE'LL COME SEE YOU PLAY ANOTHER TIME.

WHAT A BEAUTIFUL PALACE, MR. DE NOLHAC!

OH MY, MR. DE NOLHAC, ALL OF PARIS IS IN VERSAILLES!

THINK WHATEVER YOU WANT, HENRI, BUT TO FATHER, VERSAILLES WILL ALWAYS COME BEFORE US.

YOU'LL SEE!

VERSAILLES. THE EVENING OF SEPTEMBER 16, 1902.

WHAT DO YOU THINK, PIERRE?

I'M TERRIFIED-- EVEN THE SLIGHTEST FAUX PAS WILL BE POINTED OUT.

YOU KNOW, I'M TIRED OF ALL THESE RECEPTIONS...

DON'T BE SILLY, YOU LOOK VERY BEAUTIFUL.

BESIDES, I CAN'T AFFORD TO MISS SUCH AN EVENING.

THE CRÈME DE LA CRÈME OF PARIS WILL BE PRESENT, A UNIQUE OPPORTUNITY!

OH, YOU AND YOUR STREAMER OF CELEBRITIES TO MEET!

IT FEELS LIKE THERE ARE MANY OF THESE "UNIQUE OPPORTUNITIES."

AND THIS BONI DE CASTELLANE, WHAT'S HE LIKE?

I'VE HEARD SO MUCH ABOUT HIM.

HE'S AN ECCENTRIC.

FRIENDLY, IN ANY CASE.

AFTER PHARAONIC CONSTRUCTION WORK, BONIFACE DE CASTELLANE INAUGURATED HIS "PINK PALACE," INSPIRED BY THE GRAND TRIANON, WITH GREAT POMP AND CIRCUMSTANCE.

THERE WERE POLITICIANS, ARTISTS, WEALTHY AMERICAN FRANCOPHILES...

GOOD EVENING, DEAR FRIENDS. YOU'RE HERE AT LAST! WELCOME TO MY PALACE!

MADAME.

GOOD EVENING, DEAR BONI.

SO, WHAT DO YOU THINK OF MY AMBASSADORS' STAIRCASE?!*

*THE AMBASSADORS' STAIRCASE, BUILT IN VERSAILLES UNDER THE REIGN OF LOUIS XIV, WAS DESTROYED IN 1752.

93

WELL--

AND YOU HAVEN'T HAD A CHANCE TO ADMIRE THE PINK FACADE ON AVENUE DU BOIS.

I HAD IT BUILT ON THE MODEL OF THE GRAND TRIANON OF VERSAILLES!

YOU'LL HAVE TO COME BACK IN THE DAYTIME.

YES, OF COURSE WE'LL BE BACK!

PERFECT! LET'S GO UPSTAIRS AND HAVE SOME CHAMPAGNE!

GORDON BENNETT IS ALREADY UP THERE WITH OUR FRIENDS FROM THE NEW WORLD.

AN OPPORTUNITY FOR MY WIFE, ANNA,* TO SPEAK HER MOTHER TONGUE.

THE PALACE WAS ON EVERYONE'S LIPS--IT'S FASHION TRANSCENDED BORDERS. BUT PAOLO WAS RIGHT, EVERYTHING COMES WITH A PRICE. AND MY MOTHER HAD TO PAY IT.

*THE PARISIAN DANDY BONIFACE DE CASTELLANE MARRIED ANNA GOULD, A RICH AMERICAN HEIRESS, IN NEW YORK IN 1895. LEGEND HAS IT THAT THE COUNT SAID THESE WORDS ABOUT HIS WIFE: *ELLE EST TRES BELLE...VUE DE DOT*, WHICH IS A PLAY ON WORDS USING THE FRENCH HOMOPHONES "DOT" AND "DOS" SOUNDING LIKE, "SHE'S BEAUTIFUL...SEEN FROM THE BACK," BUT WRITTEN AS, "SHE'S BEAUTIFUL...SEEN FROM HER DOWRY."

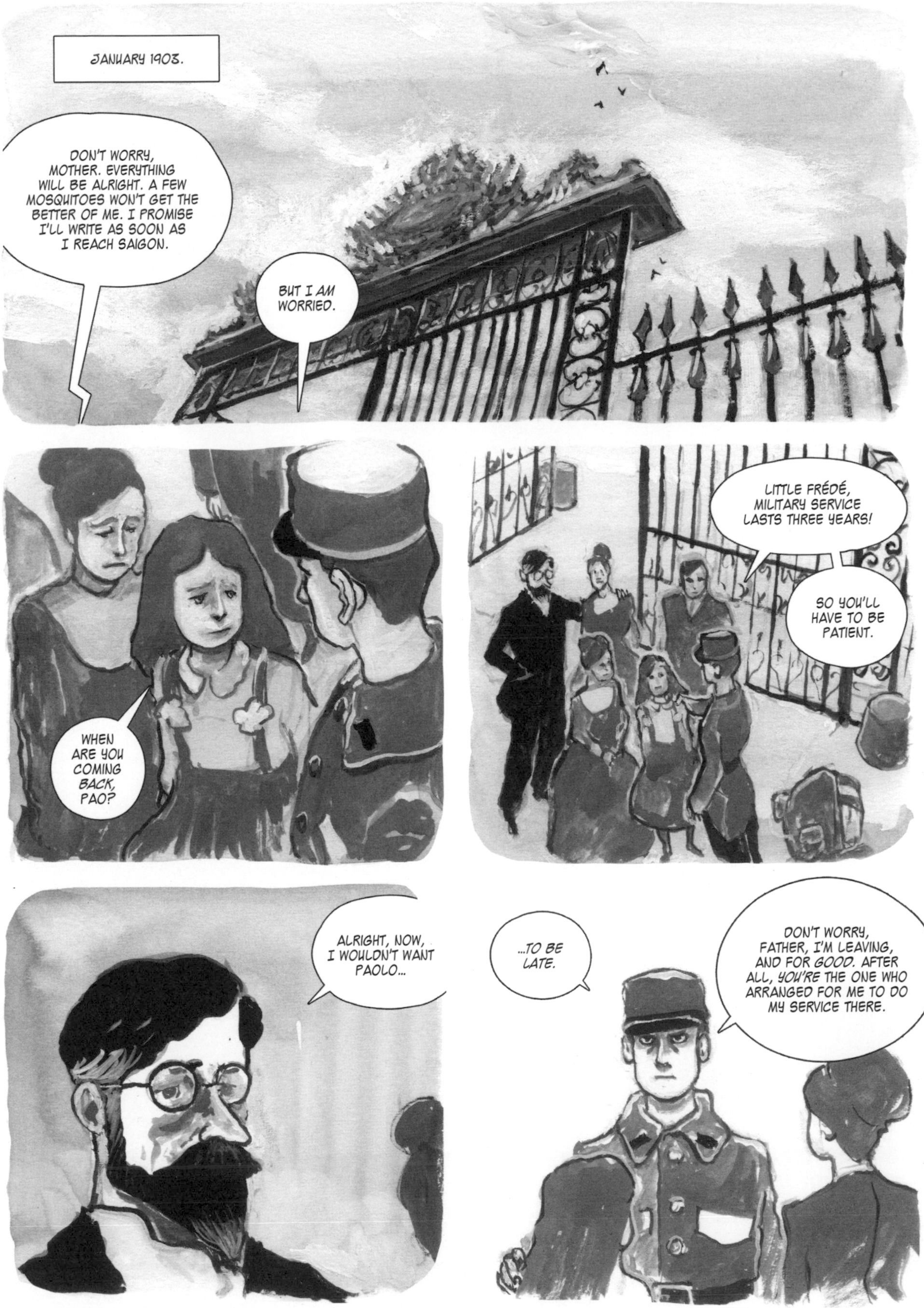

JANUARY 1903.
DON'T WORRY, MOTHER. EVERYTHING WILL BE ALRIGHT. A FEW MOSQUITOES WON'T GET THE BETTER OF ME. I PROMISE I'LL WRITE AS SOON AS I REACH SAIGON.
BUT I AM WORRIED.
WHEN ARE YOU COMING BACK, PAO?
LITTLE FRÉDÉ, MILITARY SERVICE LASTS THREE YEARS!
SO YOU'LL HAVE TO BE PATIENT.
ALRIGHT, NOW, I WOULDN'T WANT PAOLO...
...TO BE LATE.
DON'T WORRY, FATHER, I'M LEAVING, AND FOR GOOD. AFTER ALL, YOU'RE THE ONE WHO ARRANGED FOR ME TO DO MY SERVICE THERE.

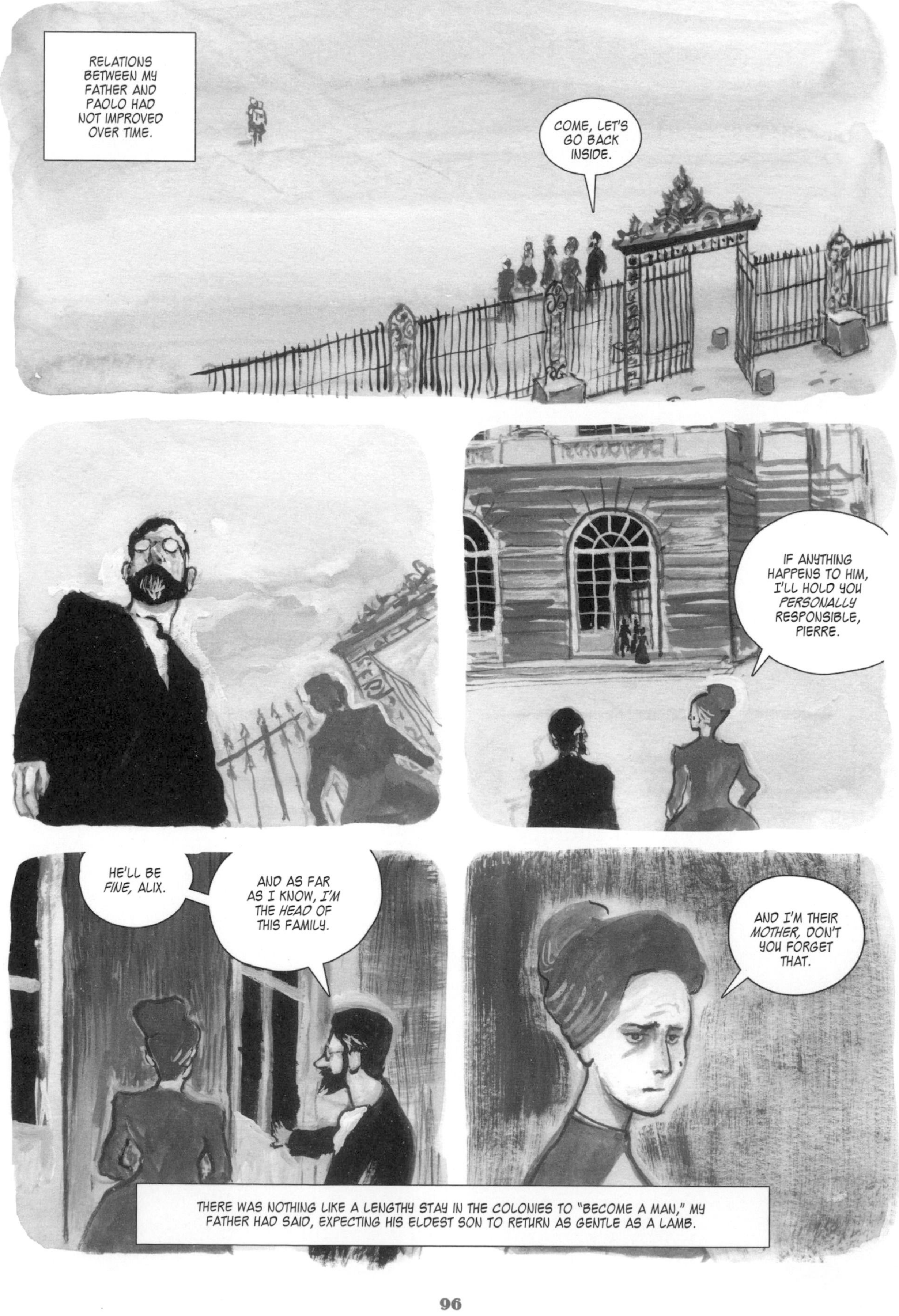
RELATIONS BETWEEN MY FATHER AND PAOLO HAD NOT IMPROVED OVER TIME.
COME, LET'S GO BACK INSIDE.
IF ANYTHING HAPPENS TO HIM, I'LL HOLD YOU *PERSONALLY* RESPONSIBLE, PIERRE.
HE'LL BE *FINE*, ALIX.
AND AS FAR AS I KNOW, *I'M* THE *HEAD* OF THIS FAMILY.
AND I'M THEIR *MOTHER*, DON'T YOU FORGET THAT.
THERE WAS NOTHING LIKE A LENGTHY STAY IN THE COLONIES TO "BECOME A MAN," MY FATHER HAD SAID, EXPECTING HIS ELDEST SON TO RETURN AS GENTLE AS A LAMB.

PARIS, 9 RUE DELAMBRE. AUTUMN OF 1935.

KNOCK KNOCK KNOCK

HELLO, MOTHER.

HELLO, MARIE-LOUISE.

MOTHER...

FATHER'S HEALTH IS GETTING WORSE.

YES, I KNOW, YOUR BROTHER ALREADY TOLD ME.

I DON'T KNOW IF...

MAYBE YOU SHOULD...

MY SWEET CHILD, DON'T BE AFRAID, I KNOW EXACTLY WHAT I HAVE TO DO...

VERSAILLES.
DECEMBER 23, 1905.

WOULDN'T THAT BE *WONDERFUL*, MR. DE NOLHAC?

YES, OF COURSE.

JUST IMAGINE... TOGETHER, WE COULD CREATE THE "FRENCH BAYREUTH."

MY DEAR COUNTESS GREFFULHE, I AM DELIGHTED AT THE THOUGHT OF THE OPERA OF VERSAILLES RETURNING TO ITS ORIGINAL PURPOSE.

BUT, AS YOU KNOW, THE MEMBERS OF PARLIAMENT ARE IN CHARGE OF IT, AND THEY WON'T BE EASY TO CONVINCE, *BELIEVE ME.*

WE ARE HARDLY ALLOWED TO ENTER IT WITHOUT THEM.

AN URGENT TELEGRAM FOR YOU, MR. DE NOLHAC.

THANK YOU.

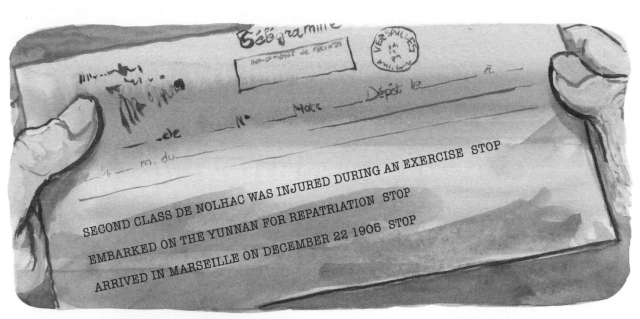

SECOND CLASS DE NOLHAC WAS INJURED DURING AN EXERCISE STOP

EMBARKED ON THE YUNNAN FOR REPATRIATION STOP

ARRIVED IN MARSEILLE ON DECEMBER 22 1905 STOP

IS EVERYTHING ALRIGHT?

NO.

I'M SORRY, COUNTESS, I HAVE TO GO... A FAMILY EMERGENCY.

PAOLO?

HELLO, FATHER.

BUT...

BUT THE TELEGRAM SAID...

... HOW ARE YOU?

I'M WELL, FATHER.

I BROKE MY LEG IN THE DELTA, AND THEN I GOT MALARIA.

FATHER, I'D LIKE YOU TO MEET SOMEONE.

THIS IS LUCIE LORRAIN.

WE MET IN SAIGON, AT THE CENTRAL POST OFFICE.

WE WANT TO GET MARRIED AND MOVE TO AMERICA.

PAOLO, DID I HEAR THAT RIGHT?

YOU DID INDEED, PIERRE.

WE'RE GOING TO CELEBRATE THE FAMILY'S *FIRST* MARRIAGE.

MY BELOVED NEPHEW, A MARRIED MAN!

ALIX, THIS WEDDING, AMERICA, IT'S *MADNESS!*

AND MY SISTER, TAKING *YOUR* SIDE!

OUR ELDEST SON HAS BECOME A MAN, PIERRE.

IT'S WHAT YOU WANTED, ISN'T IT?

HE CAME BACK SAFE AND SOUND, THAT'S WHAT MATTERS.

AND SHE SEEMS LIKE A NICE GIRL.

RIGHT, WELL, NOT IF I HAVE SOMETHING TO SAY ABOUT IT.

VERSAILLES, NOVEMBER 1906.

THIS MEETING WITH THE NEW SUB-DIRECTOR OF THE BEAUX-ARTS, HENRI DUJARDIN-BEAUMETZ, IS CRUCIAL TO INITIATE THE REBIRTH OF THE GRAND TRIANON.

WE MUST GIVE MR. DE CASTELLANE CREDIT FOR MAKING THIS PALACE POPULAR BY BUILDING HIS PARISIAN REPLICA!

AND NOW THAT VERSAILLES AND THE ENTIRE ESTATE HAVE BEEN CLASSIFIED AS *HISTORIC MONUMENTS*...

...WE HAVE AN ADDITIONAL ARGUMENT FOR CONVINCING THE GOVERNMENT TO GRANT US FUNDS.

ALRIGHT, I HAVE TO GO, I DON'T WANT TO KEEP HIM WAITING.

MY FATHER SOMETIMES DID THINGS AS THEY CAME ALONG. ESPECIALLY SINCE HE KNEW LITTLE ABOUT THIS NEWLY APPOINTED SUB-DIRECTOR OF THE BEAUX-ARTS. HE HAD MANAGED TO TAKE ADVANTAGE OF THE PRESS TO PROMOTE VERSAILLES, BUT HE FOUND OUT THAT THIS WEAPON COULD ALSO BE USED AGAINST HIM.

SIX MONTHS LATER, WORK
ON THE GRAND TRIANON
STILL HADN'T STARTED...

FOR ONCE, MY MOTHER HAD MANAGED
TO CONVINCE MY FATHER TO CHANGE HIS MIND,
AND PAOLO AND LUCIE'S WEDDING TOOK
PLACE IN MAY OF 1907.

NATURALLY, MY BROTHER HAD
INSISTED THAT THE PALACE NOT
BE SEEN IN THE FAMILY PHOTO.

VERSAILLES.
JUNE 24, 1907.

IN LESS THAN TEN MINUTES, MR. DE NOLHAC, YOU WILL BE ABLE TO MAKE THE FIRST TELEPHONE CALL IN THE HISTORY OF THE PALACE OF VERSAILLES!

OH, FRÉDÉ, QUICK! GO GET MOTHER!

NOW, NOW, GIRLS. I DON'T THINK IT'S NECESSARY TO DISTURB YOUR MOTHER FOR THAT.

THANK YOU, GENTLEMEN.

DON'T FORGET TO LEAVE US THE INSTRUCTIONS MANUAL!

NOW I CAN CALL MY COLLEAGUES AT THE LOUVRE WITHOUT HAVING TO GO TO RUE DE RIVOLI!

HELLOOO, GEORGES-HENRI?

SURE, WE CAN MEET UP TONIGHT...

HEE HEE HEE...

105

*RAYMOND POINCARÉ (1860-1934) WAS A CENTER-RIGHT STATESMAN WHO HAS BEEN BOTH PRIME MINISTER AND PRESIDENT OF FRANCE (1913-1920). ALEXANDRE MILLERAND (1859-1943), WAS ONE OF POINCARÉ'S POLITICAL RIVALS ON THE FAR-LEFT SIDE OF THE BOARD. HE BECAME PRESIDENT AFTER HIM (1920-1924) BUT BOTH MEN GOVERNED TOGETHER AS POINCARÉ BECAME PRIME MINISTER UNDER HIS TENURE.

VERSAILLES. SEPTEMBER 1909.

MR. DE VAL AND I ARE FORCED TO ADMIT IT, MY FRIEND... YOUR HUSBAND WORKED *MIRACLES* AT VERSAILLES.

YES--

SOAK IT UP! WE *RARELY* ADMIT OUR WRONGS...

MADAME du BARRY

par Claude Saint-André

Préface de Pierre de Nolhac

WILL YOU LOOK AT THAT!

"CLAUDE!" ALIX, I SUPPOSE YOU KNOW WHO'S HIDING BEHIND THIS ALIAS?

ALIX?!

ANDRÉ, WOULD YOU EXCUSE ME, I HAVE TO SPEAK WITH MY HUSBAND.

WHAT'S ALL THE FUSS ABOUT, ALIX?

WE'VE ALREADY FALLEN WAY BEHIND SCHEDULE FOR OUR NEXT EXHIBITION AND THE CUSTODIANS' STRIKE HASN'T HELPED.

HOW COULD YOU, PIERRE?

I SAW THE BOOK YOU PREFACED...

OH! IF *THAT'S* ALL IT IS...

...THEN I'M *RELIEVED*.

EVERYONE IS AWARE...

...EVEN MRS. DE VAL, THAT *CLAUDE SAINT-ANDRÉ* IS IN FACT MADAME DE *LATXAGUE!*

MY HUSBAND, WORKING WITH *ANOTHER* WOMAN!

I *NEVER* WOULD HAVE THOUGHT YOU'D BE ABLE TO *INSULT* ME LIKE THIS!

*ORGANIZATION DEDICATED TO REDUCING INFANT MORTALITY, NOTABLY BY DISTRIBUTING STERILIZED MILK TO MOTHERS WHO COULD NOT BREASTFEED THEIR CHILD.

110

A FEW DAYS LATER, MY MOTHER LEFT MY FATHER FOR GOOD. OR PERHAPS IT WAS THE OTHER WAY AROUND. IT DOESN'T MATTER...

TRUTH WAS,
THE PALACE HAD WON.

PARIS. DECEMBER 24, 1909.

OFFICIAL OPENING
JANUARY 9, 1910

MY PARENTS AGREED TO AVOID CREATING ANY SCANDALS. THEY WOULD NOT DIVORCE.

MY FATHER HAD RENTED AN APARTMENT FOR MY MOTHER ON RUE DELAMBRE.

MOTHER...

I HAVE SOME WONDERFUL NEWS FOR YOU.

WHAT IS IT, MARIE-LOUISE?

GEORGES-HENRI ASKED FATHER FOR MY HAND IN MARRIAGE YESTERDAY.

MOTHER, I DIDN'T MEAN TO MAKE YOU CRY.

PLEASE FORGIVE ME...

THAT'S *TERRIFIC*, SWEETHEART. *CONGRATULATIONS.*

VERSAILLES. THE NEXT DAY.

MY CHILDREN...

I WOULD LIKE TO PROPOSE A TOAST TO YOUR SISTER'S HAPPINESS.

AND A MERRY CHRISTMAS!

ARE YOU ALRIGHT, FATHER?

YES, YES, HENRI, THANK YOU. IT'S NOTHING, IT'LL PASS.

THE FIRST CHRISTMAS WITHOUT YOUR MOTHER...

THE VERY SAME YEAR MY SWEET SISTER PASSES AWAY.

HERE, FATHER.

MERRY CHRISTMAS!

*THIS PAINTING WAS ADDED TO THE PALACE OF VERSAILLES' COLLECTION ON NOVEMBER 30, 1936. IT IS NOW ON DISPLAY IN ONE OF THE GRAND COMMUN'S ROOMS.

VERSAILLES NOW HAD ITS OWN LUXURY HOTEL, SO AS TO ACCOMMODATE BOTH THE PARISIAN INTELLIGENTSIA AND WEALTHY TOURISTS PROPERLY.

*THE ZOUAVE IS A STATUE ON THE PONT DE L'ALMA BRIDGE. IT IS INFORMALLY USED TO MEASURE THE SEINE'S TIDE.

1912.

IN VERSAILLES, AS IN ANY PLACE, SOME YEARS SEEMED TO GO BY FASTER THAN OTHERS.

THE ARCHITECT MARCEL LAMBERT HAD LEFT THE PALACE FOR THE ARCHDIOCESE OF TOURS, WHICH PLEASED MY FATHER. BENJAMIN CHAUSSEMICHE HAD REPLACED HIM.

MARIE-LOUISE HAD BECOME MRS. SALVY.

EUGÈNE HAD BEEN APPOINTED CHIEF CUSTODIAN AND WAS NOW IN CHARGE OF SUPERVISING THE NEW RECRUITS.

TWO ENGLISH WOMEN HAD WRITTEN A BEST-SELLING BOOK ABOUT THEIR PARANORMAL ENCOUNTER WITH THE GHOST OF MARIE-ANTOINETTE...

...AND THE TITANIC HAD SUNK, ITS "VERSAILLES" LOUNGE ALONG WITH IT.

PAOLO AND LUCIE HAD RETURNED BANKRUPT FROM AMERICA WITH FOUR CHILDREN.

JANUARY 17, 1913, EARLY MORNING.

EVERY SEVEN YEARS, THE NATIONAL ASSEMBLY GATHERED IN VERSAILLES TO ELECT THE NEW PRESIDENT OF THE REPUBLIC.

HONORABLE MEMBERS, PLEASE BE SILENT.

TAP
TAP
TAP

WE WILL NOW ANNOUNCE THE RESULTS OF THE VOTE!

WITH 492 VOTES...

...I HEREBY DECLARE RAYMOND NICOLAS LANDRY POINCARÉ, PRESIDENT OF THE COUNCIL AND MINISTER OF FOREIGN AFFAIRS, TO BE ELECTED TENTH PRESIDENT OF THE FRENCH REPUBLIC, ON THIS DAY, JANUARY 17, 1913, IN VERSAILLES.

MY FATHER WAS AN INTRUDER ALLOWED TO CONTEMPLATE THIS POLITICAL COMMOTION. HE MET GEORGES CLÉMENCEAU THERE.

DE NOLHAC, MY FEARS HAVE BECOME REALITY: JULES PAMS HAS BEEN DEFEATED.

I'M WORRIED THAT OUR NEW PRESIDENT'S MODERATION WILL BE DETRIMENTAL TO FRANCE.

CLÉMENCEAU WAS RIGHT TO BE WORRIED. UNDER THE CHEERS OF THE CROWD, IN VERSAILLES, BEGAN A SEVEN-YEAR TERM DESTINED FOR TRAGEDY. A TRAGEDY THAT WOULD SPARE NEITHER THE PALACE NOR THE DE NOLHACS.

HOORAY!

CLAP!

CLAP!

CLAP!

LONG LIVE THE NEW PRESIDENT!

Chapter 4
VERSAILLES BETWEEN WAR AND PEACE

VERSAILLES. JULY 31, 1914.

IT SEEMS TO HAVE HANDLED THE TRIP FROM THE NATIONAL LIBRARY JUST FINE, MR. DE NOLHAC.

GOOD, WE'LL BE ABLE TO DISPLAY THEM.

EUGÈNE, GENTLEMEN, WE'RE GOING TO UNPACK THE SECOND GLOBE SO THAT MR. DURANDEAU MAY EXAMINE IT.

THE NEXT DAY, THE CORONELLI* GLOBE EXHIBITION AT THE PALACE WAS NO LONGER ON THE AGENDA. MILITARY ESCALATION WAS UNDERWAY. GERMANY HAD DECLARED WAR ON RUSSIA, AND FRANCE WAS MOBILIZING. JEAN JAURÈS HAD BEEN MURDERED IN PARIS.

AS FOR ME, I WOULD SOON BE DRAFTED AS A BALLOONIST IN THE THIRD INFANTRY BATTALION.

*THE ITALIAN CARTOGRAPHER VINCENZO CORONELLI CREATED TWO GIANT GLOBES FOR LOUIS XIV. KEPT AT THE NATIONAL LIBRARY OF FRANCE, THEY DEPICT THE STATE OF THE WORLD AND THE HEAVENS AT THE END OF THE SEVENTEENTH CENTURY.

AUGUST 3, 1914.

GENTLEMEN...

...TODAY, GERMANY HAS DECLARED WAR ON FRANCE.

THE PREFECT HAS JUST ORDERED THE PALACE TO BE CLOSED IMMEDIATELY.

YOU ARE CALLED UPON TO DEFEND OUR COUNTRY, AND I AM CONFIDENT THAT YOU WILL PUT AS MUCH HEART AND COURAGE INTO IT AS YOU HAVE ALL THESE YEARS AT THE SERVICE OF THIS PALACE.

YOU CAN BE SURE THAT OUR THOUGHTS WILL BE WITH YOU THROUGHOUT THIS WAR, WHICH WE HOPE WILL BE AS BRIEF AS POSSIBLE.

THANK YOU, GENTLEMEN.

RING RING RING

HELLO?

YES, ALIX, THE THREE OF THEM ARE HERE.

THEIR MILITARY PASSBOOK INDICATES VERSAILLES AS THE PLACE OF MOBILIZATION.

EUGÈNE, THE CONSERVATION ATTACHÉS, AND THE CUSTODIANS LEFT YESTERDAY.

MY FATHER WAS UNDENIABLY A TOUGH MAN.

YOU HAVE TO *UNDERSTAND*, ALIX, THAT THIS IS *WAR*.

AN UNCOMPROMISING AUVERGNE NATIVE, SHAPED BY HIS EDUCATION AND HIS TIME.

BUT I DON'T THINK THAT KEPT HIM FROM WORRYING ABOUT HIS TWO SONS, HIS SON-IN-LAW, AND HIS TEAMS, WHO WERE ALL GOING TO WAR.

SEPTEMBER 5, 1914.

THE NEWS FROM THE FRONT IS BAD, ANDRÉ.

THE GERMANS ARE ADVANCING AT AN ALARMING SPEED.

RAYMOND POINCARÉ LEFT WITH THE GOVERNMENT FOR BORDEAUX ON TUESDAY.

CLÉMENCEAU STAYED IN PARIS.

I PHONED THE LOUVRE THIS MORNING.

THEY ARE RELOCATING THEIR MASTERPIECES TO THE SOUTH WITH A SPECIAL TRAIN.

THEY CAN ARRANGE TO HAVE A WAGON FOR THE PALACE IF NEED BE.

WE HAVE TWENTY-FOUR HOURS TO DECIDE.

EVERYONE WAS AFRAID THAT THE GERMANS WOULD OCCUPY THE COUNTRY AS THEY HAD IN 1870.

WE CAN HIDE THE PIECES THAT ARE STAYING DOWN HERE IN THIS PALACE CELLAR.

I'LL SEAL IT OFF WITH MORTAR, THE GERMANS WILL NEVER FIND THEM.

LET'S GO BACK UPSTAIRS AND LOAD THE MASTERPIECES INTO THE TRUCK FIRST.

THE DRIVER HAS TO BE AT GARE DE LYON STATION AT EIGHT O'CLOCK TOMORROW MORNING.

MARIE-ANTOINETTE WITH A ROSE...

SIX GOBELIN TAPESTRIES...

THE BOULLE DESK.

CHECK.

CHECK.

CHECK.

THAT'S ALL OF IT!

I WANT *YOU* TO ESCORT THEM TO THE SOUTH, ANDRÉ.

OUR TREASURES ARE IN YOUR HANDS. DRIVE CAREFULLY.

HAVE MONSIEUR PÉRATÉ CALL ME FROM THE GARE DE LYON.

VERSAILLES' MASTERPIECES ARRIVED SAFELY.

THEY STAYED THERE THROUGHOUT THE ENTIRE WAR, WHICH LASTED MUCH LONGER THAN EXPECTED.

SPRING OF 1915.

MR. PIERRE?

YES, ERNESTINE, WHAT IS IT?

YOUR DAUGHTER, MRS. FRÉDÉRIQUE, IS IN THE HALLWAY.

HOW NICE OF YOU TO COME AND VISIT YOUR FATHER, MY FRÉDÉ.

UNFORTUNATELY, I HAVE VERY LITTLE TIME. I HAVE TO OPEN UP THE PALACE TO WELCOME THE WOUNDED SOLDIERS RETURNING FROM THE FRONT. PREFECT'S ORDERS.

THESE POOR MEN HAVE EARNED A DAY OF ENTERTAINMENT.

WELL, THAT'S JUST IT, FATHER, I'M HERE TO HELP YOU.

I WANT TO WORK AT THE PALACE.

DID I HEAR THAT RIGHT?

ABSOLUTELY, FATHER.

NEARLY ALL THE MEN HAVE LEFT, YOU ARE SORELY UNDERSTAFFED. SO HERE I AM.

THE WAR EFFORT, DOES THAT RING A BELL?

EUGÈNE'S WIFE IS YOUR SECRETARY, IS SHE NOT?

I CAN DO ANYTHING, WHATEVER THE PALACE NEEDS--

BUT, FRÉDÉRIQUE, A WOMAN OF *YOUR* RANK MUSTN'T WORK.

I'LL BET THIS WAS *YOUR* MOTHER'S IDEA.

YOU'RE MISTAKEN.

I'M TWENTY-TWO, I CAN MAKE MY OWN DECISIONS!

BUT IF YOU DON'T WANT MY HELP, THEN I'LL WORK IN THE TRIANON PALACE'S ENGLISH INFIRMARY...

...THEY'RE LOOKING FOR VOLUNTEERS TO TAKE CARE OF THE WOUNDED *BRITISH* SOLDIERS.

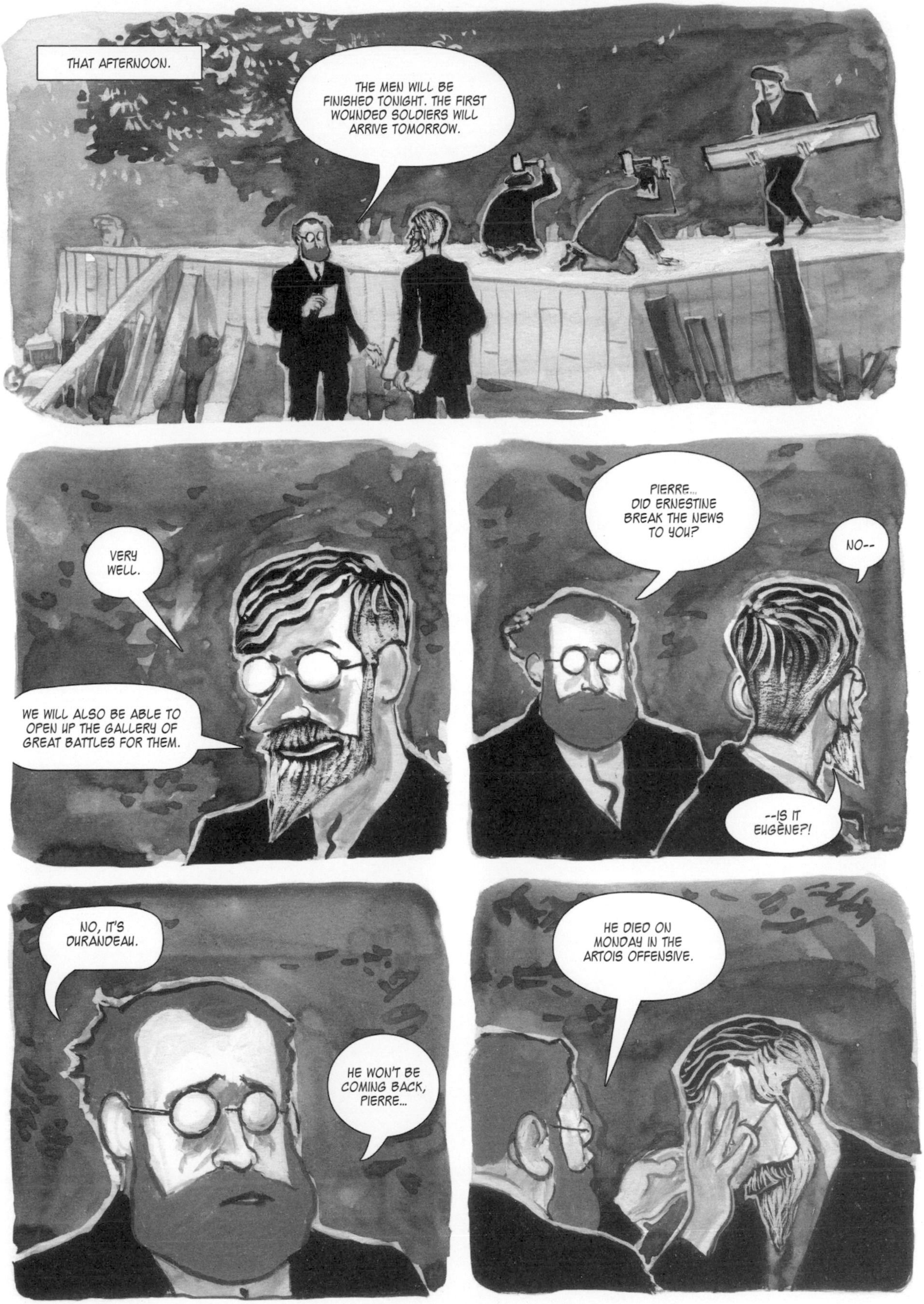
THAT AFTERNOON.
THE MEN WILL BE FINISHED TONIGHT. THE FIRST WOUNDED SOLDIERS WILL ARRIVE TOMORROW.
VERY WELL.
WE WILL ALSO BE ABLE TO OPEN UP THE GALLERY OF GREAT BATTLES FOR THEM.
PIERRE... DID ERNESTINE BREAK THE NEWS TO YOU?
NO--
--IS IT EUGÈNE?!
NO, IT'S DURANDEAU.
HE WON'T BE COMING BACK, PIERRE...
HE DIED ON MONDAY IN THE ARTOIS OFFENSIVE.

June 1915

My Dear Henri,

I'm writing to check up on you. Every day we get terrible news from the front. The endemic mud in the trenches, the nightly assaults, food rationing, diseases... It reassures me a little to know that you are in the rear, at your observation post in Lèzères, far from these desolate places. Our brother-in-law Georges was not as lucky and Marie-Louise is worried sick knowing that he has to carry out assault after assault. Paolo is still recovering from his injury in Val-de-Grâce,* where Lucie and the children visit him every day.

Did you receive Mother's package last month? I had put some soft caramels in there for you, the ones you love so much from Madame Casadesus at 6, Rue Royale. Do you remember how you used to bring me some when we were kids?

I've been working for over a month now at the Trianon Palace's English infirmary. I tend to the soldiers' wounds, I even give them the bottle if I need to. I'm also learning a few words of English. If you could see me waving my hands around just so some soldiers could understand me, you'd laugh so hard you'd cry.

I like this job very much, and as you can imagine, Father was opposed to it. He wants me to get married as soon as possible. But I'm not in a hurry. And thank God, Mother isn't very insistent about it.

The palace eventually reopened its doors to host charities, the wounded, the soldiers on leave from invaded countries, but everything is slow with the few custodians left who were who too old to go to battle.

Big brother, I have to go, I'm expected at the Trempignol café. All the volunteers are meeting up tonight to celebrate a soldier's miraculous recovery. There is no small victory in these difficult times.

Take care of yourself.
May God watch over you and Georges.

With all my love,
Your sister, Frédé

*THE MILITARY HOSPITAL IN PARIS.

130

DECEMBER 13, 1915.

FATHER!

GRANDFATHER!

AH, YOU'RE FINALLY HERE!

HURRY UP AND HAVE A SEAT, THE CONCERT IS ABOUT TO START.

GRANDFATHER...

WHY AREN'T YOU GOING TO WAR, TOO?

WELL, SOMEONE HAS TO TAKE CARE OF THE PALACE AND PREPARE CHRISTMAS FOR ALL THE SOLDIERS, SWEETHEART.

THANK YOU, MY DEAR SON-IN-LAW, I COULDN'T HAVE GIVEN A BETTER ANSWER MYSELF.

YESTERDAY, SHE ASKED ME IF HER OLDER BROTHER COULD GO TO THE FRONT INSTEAD OF ME.

ALLONS ENFANTS DE LA PATRIIIIE*

GEORGES-HENRI, COULD WE HAVE A WORD?

I NEED TO SPEAK WITH YOU.

*THE FRENCH NATIONAL ANTHEM.

132

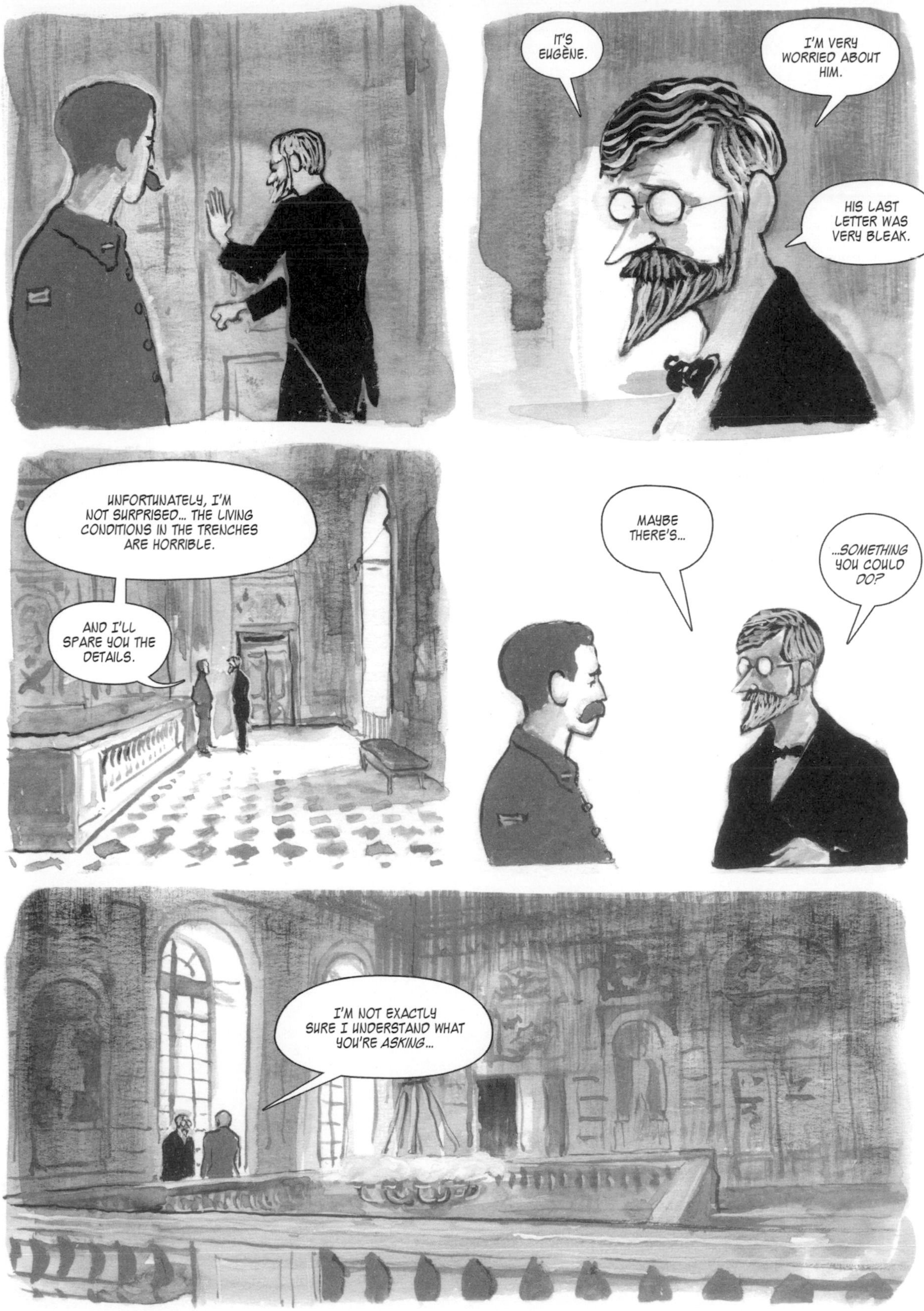
IT'S EUGÈNE.
I'M VERY WORRIED ABOUT HIM.
HIS LAST LETTER WAS VERY BLEAK.
UNFORTUNATELY, I'M NOT SURPRISED... THE LIVING CONDITIONS IN THE TRENCHES ARE HORRIBLE.
AND I'LL SPARE YOU THE DETAILS.
MAYBE THERE'S...
...SOMETHING YOU COULD DO?
I'M NOT EXACTLY SURE I UNDERSTAND WHAT YOU'RE ASKING...

I'M ASKING YOU FOR A FAVOR.

PERHAPS YOU COULD HAVE EUGÈNE ASSIGNED TO YOUR REGIMENT?

WITH ALL DUE RESPECT, I DON'T LIKE TO PROMOTE FAVORITISM.

AH, THERE YOU ARE!

WHAT ARE YOU TWO UP TO?

YOU'RE GOING TO MISS THE PRAYER FOR OUR TROOPS WHO ARE SPENDING CHRISTMAS ON THE FRONT.

MY DEAR HUSBAND, ARE YOU COMING?

I'LL SEE WHAT I CAN DO. BUT I'M JUST A SECOND LIEUTENANT.

AND, I BEG YOU, NOT A WORD TO ANYONE.

GEORGES-HENRI NEVER HAD THE OPPORTUNITY TO INTERVENE FOR EUGÈNE. HE "DIED FOR FRANCE" IN THE MEUSE.

MARIE-LOUISE WAS WIDOWED AT JUST TWENTY-FIVE YEARS OLD. WE WERE ALL DEEPLY AFFECTED.

THE WINTER OF 1917 WAS PARTICULARLY HARSH.

IT WAS INCREASINGLY DIFFICULT TO FIND FUEL FOR HEATING. THE COLD WAS DAMAGING THE MASTERPIECES, THE WOODWORK AND THE MOLDINGS...

THE PALACE NO LONGER HAD ANY FUNDING.

LOOK, ANDRÉ, IT'S ONLY FORTY DEGREES INSIDE.

VERSAILLES, WHICH MY FATHER AND ANDRÉ HAD REBUILT, WAS ONCE AGAIN, BEING GRADUALLY DISMANTLED.

SIR, YOUR APPOINTMENT HAS ARRIVED.

HELLO, SIR, GEORGES TRUFFAUT, FOUNDER OF THE TRUFFAUT GARDEN CENTER.*

MR. TRUFFAUT, AS YOU KNOW, THE PALACE OF VERSAILLES IS CONTRIBUTING TO THE WAR EFFORT.

*THE TRUFFAUT ENTERPRISE WAS FOUNDED IN VERSAILLES IN 1897 BY GEORGES TRUFFAUT, THE DESCENDANT OF A FAMILY OF GARDENERS WHO HAD BEEN WORKING FOR THE ROYAL ESTATE SINCE THE EIGHTEENTH CENTURY.

IN ADDITION TO WELCOMING THE SOLDIERS BACK FROM THE FRONT, THE PREFECT ASKED US TO USE THE ESTATE TO *GROW FOOD* FOR OUR SOLDIERS.

I'M NOT THRILLED ABOUT IT, BUT WE HAVE TO DO IT.

HM... TO CREATE A VEGETABLE GARDEN ON SEVERAL ACRES, WE'RE GOING TO NEED MANPOWER.

YES.

THE ARMY IS ASSIGNING US A REGIMENT OF SEVENTY INDOCHINESE SOLDIERS. BUT WE'RE STILL IN NEED OF RESOURCES.

HAVING SAID THAT, DO YOU THINK YOU COULD FIND US MORE WOOD SUPPLY?

I'LL SEE WHAT I CAN DO. WE'LL WORK SOMETHING OUT.

BUT YOU KNOW, NOTHING IS FREE...

IN FACT, THE PRICES ARE SOARING DUE TO THE BLACK MARKET...

THE MONTHS PASSED,
AND IT SEEMED AS THOUGH
THE WAR WOULD NEVER END.

THE INDOCHINESE WORKERS HAD BEGUN
WORKING IN THE TRIANON GARDENS.

AIR RAIDS OVER THE CAPITAL WERE
BECOMING MORE AND MORE FREQUENT
AND ALSO THREATENED VERSAILLES.

FRÉDÉRIQUE HAD FALLEN IN
LOVE WITH PIERRE BOULANGER,
A FRIEND OF PAOLO'S WHOM HE
HAD MET IN AMERICA.

I WANT YOU
FOR U.S. ARMY

AS THE SECOND BATTLE OF THE AISNE
WAS CAUSING HEAVY CASUALTIES, THE
UNITED STATES' JOINING THE WAR GAVE
THE ALLIED FORCES A LITTLE HOPE.

JANUARY 2, 1918.

HELLO, ALIX.

HELLO, PIERRE.

YOU'RE LATE.

YES, THE TRAIN GOT STUCK AT THE GARE DES CHANTIERS STATION.

FOR THE FIRST TIME SINCE 1909, MY MOTHER HAD WANTED TO SEE MY FATHER.

SO?

WHAT DO YOU INTEND TO DO?

I'M GOING TO GO TO ITALY SOON. THE UNIVERSITY OF ROME INVITED ME TO GIVE A LECTURE IN ART HISTORY.

ANDRÉ WILL REPLACE ME IN VERSAILLES, HE'S READY TO TAKE ON THIS RESPONSIBILITY.

PLEASE DON'T AVOID THE SUBJECT, PIERRE.

ARE YOU GOING TO GIVE YOUR CONSENT FOR FRÉDÉRIQUE'S WEDDING?

RESTAURANT BAR AMERICAIN A COUPOLE

I DON'T THINK SO. I'M OPPOSED TO THIS UNION.

THIS PIERRE BOULANGER IS NOT A SERIOUS MAN.

ONE DOESN'T LEAVE THE BEAUX-ARTS BEHIND TO LIVE ON ODD JOBS AND TRAVELS IN AMERICA!

OH, NOT AGAIN!

FRÉDÉRIQUE CHOSE HIM. YOU'LL LOSE YOUR DAUGHTER IF YOU PERSIST.

I HAVE A PROPOSITION TO MAKE.

*IN 1918, THE ARMY USED PONTOONS AND BRANCHES TO CAMOUFLAGE THE GRAND CANAL AND PREVENT IT FROM BEING TOO RECOGNIZABLE FROM AN AERIAL POINT OF VIEW. THE PALACE'S GLASS ROOFS WERE ALSO PAINTED TO PREVENT THEM FROM REFLECTING THE LIGHT OF THE MOON, WHICH COULD BE USED TO LOCATE THE PALACE.

JUNE 12, 1918.

MY *DEAR* PIERRE, I'M HAPPY TO SEE YOU AGAIN!

HOW WAS YOUR TRIP?

VERY GOOD.

I WAS ABLE TO RECONNECT WITH MY OLD ROMAN ACQUAINTANCES.

BUT THINGS ARE *TENSE*. THE NATIONALISTS ARE SHAKING UP THE COUNTRY.

IT SHOULD BE OKAY.

THE GERMANS ARE STRUGGLING ON THE WESTERN FRONT. GENERAL FOCH IS GOING TO WIN THIS WAR!

IN THE EVENT OF VICTORY, WE HAVE BEEN INFORMED FROM A RELIABLE SOURCE THAT THE *PEACE TREATY* WOULD BE SYMBOLICALLY SIGNED AT VERSAILLES.

AND YOU'LL BE HAPPY TO KNOW THAT WE RECEIVED A LETTER FROM EUGÈNE.

HE'S ALIVE.

141

Arras, November 12, 1918

My dear Frédé,

The bells of victory sounded all day yesterday! if only you could have seen the people come out and gather amidst the rubble of this city destroyed by the bombings. I hope I'll be demobilized soon. I'm eager to leave my uniform and the cannons behind.

Do you know when your husband will be back? I look forward to congratulating him on his War Cross that you mentioned in your last letter. I'm sure Father will be honored to have a decorated son-in-law. As you know, although he finally gave you his consent, I didn't approve of his absence from your wedding. Mother was unable to get more from him. But, just like this war, I believe that the time for peace and reconciliation will have to come. Marie-Louise will need a united family by her side to face her future.

I met a young woman on my last leave in Paris. Her name is Jeanne. I'm sure you'll like her.

See you very soon, dear sister.

Tenderly, your brother.

H. de Nolhac

JUNE 24, 1919.

LET'S GO TO THE HALL OF MIRRORS TO SEE HOW THE PREPARATIONS ARE GOING.

GEORGES CLÉMENCEAU WILL ARRIVE IN AN HOUR WITH THE PRESIDENT OF THE UNITED STATES AND THE BRITISH PRIME MINISTER...

PIERRE...

THAT DAY, AS VERSAILLES WAS GETTING READY TO HOST THE SIGNING OF THE PEACE TREATY, MY FATHER AND EUGÈNE'S REUNION WAS GRAVE AND SILENT. IT TOOK PLACE ALMOST NINE MONTHS AFTER THE ARMISTICE...

VERSAILLES.
JUNE 28, 1919.

THE BIG DAY HAD COME. THE ENTIRE WORLD WAS IN VERSAILLES FOR THE SIGNING OF THE PEACE TREATY.
THERE WERE FOREIGN DELEGATIONS, SOLDIERS, DISFIGURED VETERANS, BIG CROWDS...

MY FATHER HAD THE HEAVY
TASK OF ESCORTING THE GERMAN
PLENIPOTENTIARIES TO THE
HALL OF MIRRORS.

IT WAS ONLY AFTER HIS DEATH THAT I READ
HIS WORDS, WRITTEN IN HIS MEMOIRS.

144

"SOON, AT ONE OF THE FRENCH DOORS, BELOW THE WAR ROOM, THE GERMAN DELEGATES APPEARED.

"WHEN THE SIGNAL CAME, I WENT TO THE HEAD OF THE PROCESSION AND LEAD IT, THROUGH A SERIES OF ROOMS THAT FELT ENDLESS, TO THE MARBLE STAIRCASE.

"FOR A FEW MORE MOMENTS, THOSE WALKING BY WERE STILL THE DEFEATED ENEMY...

"AND I COULD SEE TEARS FORMING IN HERMANN MÜLLER'S* EYES.

"AS SOON AS WE APPEARED UNDER THE PEACE ROOM'S ARCADE, THE LOUD AVIARY-LIKE CHATTER STOPPED INSTANTLY: THE GERMANS WERE TAKEN TO THE SEATS RESERVED FOR THEM AND THE CEREMONY BEGAN."

*HERMANN MÜLLER, THE GERMAN FOREIGN MINISTER, WAS THE ONE WHO SIGNED THE TREATY OF VERSAILLES ON BEHALF OF HIS COUNTRY.

JANUARY 1920.

HERE YOU GO, ANDRÉ, YOU CAN NOW MOVE INTO THIS OFFICE, JUST LIKE I DID WHEN I SUCCEEDED CHARLES. YOU ARE NOW IN CHARGE.

THANK YOU, PIERRE.

BENJAMIN, MYSELF, AND EVERYONE IN VERSAILLES WILL DO OUR BEST TO PRESERVE YOUR HERITAGE... I'LL GO SEE HOW THE MOVING IS COMING ALONG.

AH, HELLO ANDRÉ.

I'M HERE TO SEE HOW FATHER'S DOING.

HE'S SORTING HIS PAST, HENRI. SEE YOU TONIGHT FOR THE SURPRISE.

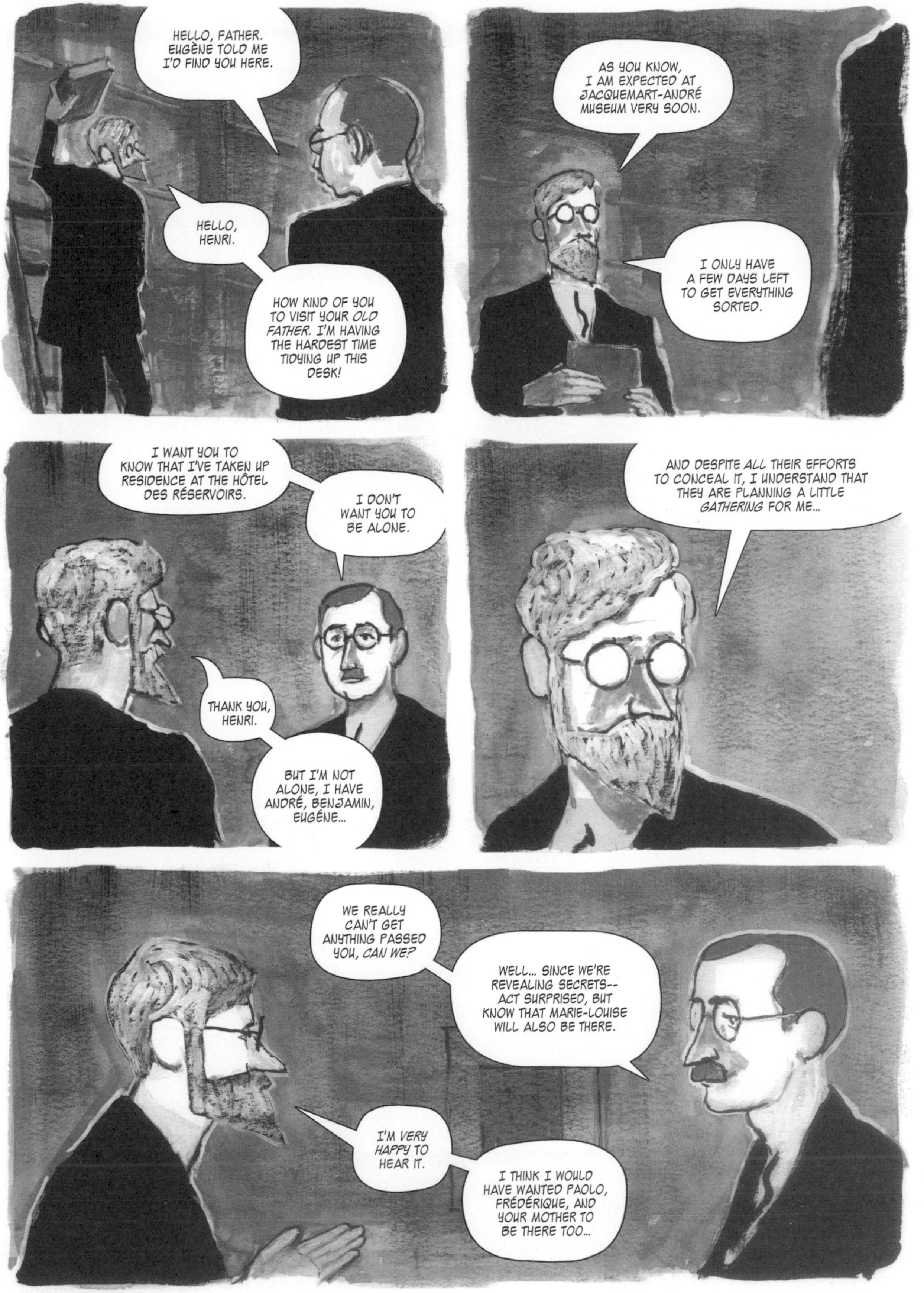

HELLO, FATHER. EUGÈNE TOLD ME I'D FIND YOU HERE.
HELLO, HENRI.
HOW KIND OF YOU TO VISIT YOUR *OLD FATHER*. I'M HAVING THE HARDEST TIME TIDYING UP THIS DESK!
AS YOU KNOW, I AM EXPECTED AT JACQUEMART-ANDRÉ MUSEUM VERY SOON.
I ONLY HAVE A FEW DAYS LEFT TO GET EVERYTHING SORTED.
I WANT YOU TO KNOW THAT I'VE TAKEN UP RESIDENCE AT THE HÔTEL DES RÉSERVOIRS.
I DON'T WANT YOU TO BE ALONE.
THANK YOU, HENRI.
BUT I'M NOT ALONE, I HAVE ANDRÉ, BENJAMIN, EUGÉNE...
AND DESPITE *ALL* THEIR EFFORTS TO CONCEAL IT, I UNDERSTAND THAT THEY ARE PLANNING A LITTLE *GATHERING* FOR ME...
WE REALLY CAN'T GET ANYTHING PASSED YOU, *CAN WE?*
WELL... SINCE WE'RE REVEALING SECRETS-- ACT SURPRISED, BUT KNOW THAT MARIE-LOUISE WILL ALSO BE THERE.
I'M *VERY HAPPY* TO HEAR IT.
I THINK I WOULD HAVE WANTED PAOLO, FRÉDÉRIQUE, AND YOUR MOTHER TO BE THERE TOO...

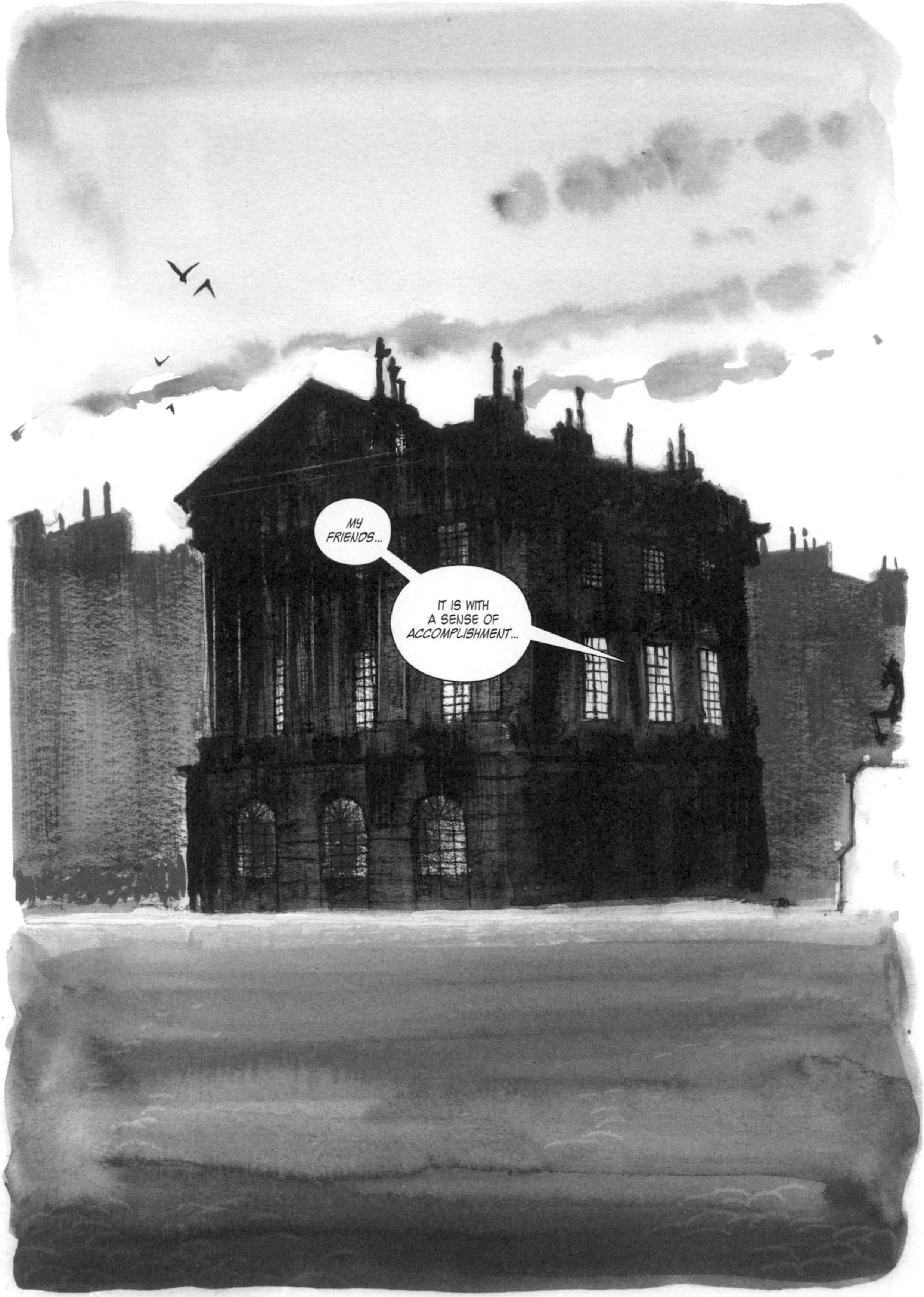
MY FRIENDS...
IT IS WITH A SENSE OF ACCOMPLISHMENT...

PARIS. JANUARY 30, 1936.

GOOD MORNING, MRS. DE NOLHAC.

THE DOCTOR RETURNED THIS MORNING TO GIVE HIM A TRANQUILIZER.

HE WAS RESTLESS ALL NIGHT.

I'D LIKE A MOMENT ALONE WITH HIM.

HE... HELLO, ALIX.

HELLO, PIERRE.

HOW ARE YOU?

IF YOU'RE HERE, THEN THAT MEANS THINGS AREN'T GOING WELL...

PIERRE, DON'T BE A *FOOL!*

IF I'M HERE, IT'S BECAUSE...

...DESPITE EVERYTHING, MY PLACE IS HERE.

YES, BEFORE I MOVE ON AND JOIN OUR FRANÇOIS AND FRÉDÉRIC.

MY FATHER DIED ON JANUARY 31, 1936,
AT THE JACQUEMART-ANDRÉ MUSEUM.
HE IS BURIED IN HIS NATIVE AUVERGNE.

IT WAS ONLY LATER THAT I DISCOVERED BY CHANCE, GOING THROUGH HIS NOTEBOOKS, THAT THE STORY OF MY FATHER'S PALACE HAD BEGUN MUCH EARLIER THAN I HAD THOUGHT.

JUNE 1878.

HE HAD COME TO VERSAILLES
THE YEAR HE TURNED EIGHTEEN...

Sunday, June 2, 1878
Traveling from Auvergne to Paris
Train at 11:34 AM

Monday the 3rd
Universal Exposition

Thursday the 6th
The Louvre Museum

Friday the 7th
Palace of Versailles

Friday the 7th
Palace of Versailles

the most beautiful place
in Paris is Versailles

VERSAILLES
My Father's Palace

DOSSIER

Portrait of Pierre de Nolhac, 1911 (Bibliothèque nationale).

This graphic novel is inspired by the memoirs of Pierre de Nolhac, published after his death in 1937. Pierre tells the story of his thirty-three years of working for the palace, something he was not intended to do. With simplicity and humor, he recounts his achievements and failures, his ambitions and doubts.

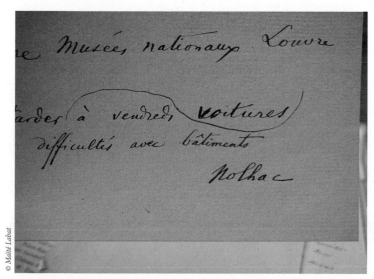

The Curator's signature (Palace of Versailles Archives).

His memoirs were a fantastic starting point, a gateway to a little-known period of the history of the Palace of Versailles. We also had to interview the curators, consult the archives, find photographs, press clippings and read everything available on the subject.

Pierre de Nolhac
de l'Académie française

LA RÉSURRECTION
DE VERSAILLES

Souvenirs d'un conservateur
1887-1920

PERRIN
La Société des Amis de Versailles

Cover of Pierre de Nolhac's memoirs, (Perrin Publishing - La Société des Amis de Versailles, November 2002).

André Pératé in 1920 (Bibliothèque nationale).

Press clipping (Municipal Library of Versailles).

*Letter from museum custodian Eugène Deziles
to Pierre de Nolhac during the First World War
(Palace of Versailles Archives).*

The Palace of Versailles, at the end of the nineteenth century. Malitte-Richard Collection (Palace of Versailles Archives).

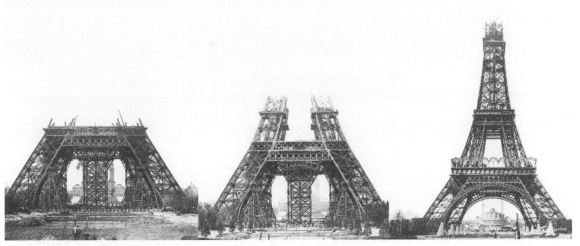

The Eiffel Tower under construction, 1888.

"DRESSING UP AS THE SUN KING... ON A RAINY DAY! HOW RIDICULOUS!"

– Georges Feydeau
Feu la mère de Madame, 1908

Une soirée au Pré-Catelan (An evening at Pré-Catelan). Oil on canvas, 1909. Outside are Anna Gould and Hélie de Talleyrand-Perigord. Inside, right bay: Marquis de Dion. Center bay: Liane de Pougy. Left bay: Santos-Dumont (Paris, Musée Carnavalet).

This research into Versailles' recent past could not be carried out without broadening our understanding of the times, of our characters' contemporaries, of the political, societal and artistic world in which they grow and age. During the Belle Époque, the Republic took root, new technologies were born, and soon thereafter changed with the advent of the First World War. Exhibitions, novels, essays, plays, films, TV series, graphic novels, history books.… For several years, we have continuously delved into what has become "our period," waltzed around it, sometimes even voluntarily moving away from the subject in order to understand it better. This is where the title *My Father's Palace* comes from, an obvious reference to Marcel Pagnol, born in 1895, only two years after Frédérique de Nolhac, who, like Henri, our narrator, tells the story of his father's and his mother's palace. Little by little, we connected the dots to understand Versailles and our characters within their times.

Soldiers gathered in the Palace of Versailles courtyard for a military parade in 1915. Malitte-Richard Collection (Palace of Versailles Archives).

James Gordon Bennett Jr., circa 1918. Founder of The International New York Times *(Harvard Theater Collection, Harvard University).*

In his memoirs, Pierre de Nolhac disregards his personal life, which blossomed and withered within that very palace. That, too, had to be researched. We obtained the most information about the de Nolhacs, about their family life in Versailles at the turn of the century, from his descendants. Claire Salvy (Marie-Louise's granddaughter), Martine Hedou (Paolo's granddaughter), Alex de La Forest (Paolo's great-grandson), Adrienne Charmet-Alix (Paolo's great-granddaughter), Solange Poulet (Henri's granddaughter) and Pascal-Henri Keller (Henri's grandson), guided us in this quest while generously sharing their family archives with us.

Henri, Alix, Paolo, François and Marie-Louise at the palace

Henri and Paolo, circa 1895 (de Nolhac Family Archives).

The de Nolhac family in 1893. In the back row, from left to right: Alix de Goys, Paul de Nolhac, Paolo and Henri (on top); Marie-Louise de Nolhac, little Marie-Louise (her goddaughter), Pierre de Nolhac. In the front row: Perrine Pacros (Claire's mother), baby Frédérique, Claire Pacros and François (de Nolhac Family Archives).

Pierre de Nolhac at the end of his life (de Nolhac Family Archives).

In this family story, we have, of course, become particularly attached to Henri de Nolhac… There are many descendants of Pierre and Alix de Nolhac and we did not have time to pursue any great genealogical ambitions, but we ran into Pascal-Henri Keller by chance and mentioned Pierre de Nolhac, who, as it turned out, was none other than his great-grandfather.…

Coincidence or fate? Freud, a contemporary of "our" period, would surely have something to say about it. In any case, this discovery was as moving as it was unexpected.

In the winter of 2019, thanks to Pascal-Henri, we had an encounter that we would never have thought possible: we met the last of Pierre de Nolhac's grandchildren who had actually known him during his lifetime. These are Pascal-Henri's mother, Élisabeth Keller, ninety-seven years old, and his uncle, Jean, ninety-one years old, the last of the de Nolhacs.

Uncle Jean's mailbox in Paris.

*Henri de Nolhac, photo booth picture, January 1929
(de Nolhac Family Archives).*

Pierre de Nolhac's descendants also granted us unconditional access to the archives inherited from Henri, who became a painter, draftsman and illustrator. Here is some of his work in his family's possession, as well as his portrait of Pierre de Nolhac, which remains in the Palace of Versailles' collection.

Pierre de Nolhac painted by his son Henri, 1909
(Palace of Versailles).

Paolo in 1902, drawn by his brother Henri
(de Nolhac Family Archives).

Marie-Louise in Versailles, by Henri de Nolhac, 1905
(de Nolhac Family Archives).

Marie-Louise in 1902, drawn by her brother Henri
(de Nolhac Family Archives).

First sketches of the palace by Alexis Vitrebert.

This long documentary journey served two purposes: the creation of the narrative and the gathering of iconographic sources for its illustration. At the start of the project, Alexis Vitrebert knew little about Versailles and even less about Pierre de Nolhac, this illustrious yet unknown figure. However, thanks to all this documentation—and after a long visit to the palace—he was able to make the story's sites and protagonists his own from the start.

He immediately got to work: on the one hand his sketches, on the other hand his research on the final aesthetics of the plates. The project took shape, and Pierre came to life.

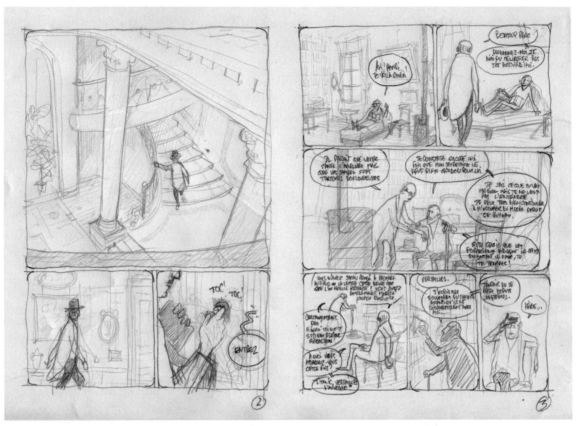

Sketches of plates 2 and 3.

This story was always intended to be a graphic novel, and it became obvious one day that it had to be told in black and white. Everything pointed us in that direction. For Alexis, opting for gouache was a revelation, and ink wash replaced the originally intended line drawings. This technique allowed him to capture immediacy, depths of field, emotions, shades and nuances.

Excerpt from plate 9.

This choice was not entirely a coincidence. As a child, in the 1980s, Alexis was influenced by cartoons, especially those from Studio Ghibli in Tokyo, where Hayao Miyazaki's films were made. There, the decors were painted with gouache. As for Alexis, he worked on the originals with a paintbrush in his studio.

There is always an element of fiction when telling a true story—these voluntary, unconscious or omitted white lies with which we work, just like in real life. We coined the term "fictional freedoms," and wanted them to be realistic at all times. Yves Carlier, Chief Curator at the Palace of Versailles, was kind enough to help us find this delicate balance throughout the project. These freedoms have served to give rhythm to the narrative or fill in the gaps that history has left open, while taking care not to distort the reality of our characters and the setting too much.

And so we gradually pieced together how Versailles had, thanks to Pierre de Nolhac, reclaimed its place in history, its share of light. The scriptwriters and the illustrator did not want to tell the story of the Versailles of kings, but that of the Republic, the one that has been explored by its visitors for a little over a century now.

– Maïté L.

© Maud Modjo

ACKNOWLEDGEMENTS

Someone once said, "making a movie borders on a miracle." This graphic novel was also very lucky, particularly because it was well supported. We want to thank those who made this project possible and who developed it with us, day by day: Vincent Henry, our publisher, Morgane Hébert, Morgane Jandot and the entire *La Boîte à Bulles* team.

Stéphane Lemardelé for his precious storyboards at the final stages of the project.

Those at the Palace of Versailles who supported the project: Catherine Pégard, Laurent Salomé, Thierry Gausseron, Louis-Samuel Berger. The publishing department headed by Jean-Vincent Bacquart, and particularly Anne Carasso, publisher, who was with us throughout the creative process, but also Marie Leimbacher, publisher, who was with us from the start. Yves Carlier, Chief Curator, expert on Pierre de Nolhac and on the palace at that time. Ariane de Lestrange, Mathilde Brunel, Hélène Dalifard, Violaine Solari, Elsa Martin, Élise Albenque, Thomas Garnier, Jérémie Le Guillou, Ghania Sahlioui, Christian Milet and the entire communication team, who were the first to lend their belief in this project. Marie-Laëtitia Lachèvre, Delphine Valmalle, Claire Bonnotte, Karine McGrath who shared their research and knowledge. And all the teams at the Palace of Versailles for their contribution and encouragement.

Emmanuel Guibert and Béatrix Saule for their valuable advice. The Lemarié family, who knows why. Claire Salvy, Pascal-Henri Keller, Jean de Nolhac, Élisabeth Keller, Martine Hedou, Alex de La Forest, Adrienne Charmet-Alix and Solange Poulet for their generosity. The archive centers and their teams, for opening their doors to allow us to conduct our research, in particular the Versailles Public Library.

A big thanks to Pauline for all her proofreading and corrections, and to all who were on the front lines for this project: Maxime, Mathilde, Romain, Nico, Louis, Hélène, Monica, Agnès et Nadeige, to my parents and my family, to my friends an everybody who supported me, to my accomplices at the Louvre, in Versailles and elsewhere.

– Maïté Labat

Thanks to my partner Jenny, my friends at the studio, Johann, Simon, Simon, Caps, Margaux, Karine, David and a big special thanks to Maud for her proofreading and cover models, to my parents, to Sylvette, to my brothers and my family, to Loïc for the light table and to all those who supported me in any way!

– Alexis Vitrebert

A big thank you to Maïté, Romain, Vincent, Alexis, the teams at La Boîte à Bulles and at the Palace of Versailles, for having taken me on this adventure, my wife Virginie, my family and my friends for having advised, inspired and supported me!

– Jean-Baptiste Veber

SELECTED BIBLIOGRAPHY

• *La Résurrection de Versailles. Souvenirs d'un conservateur, 1887-1920,* Pierre de Nolhac. Paris: Plon, 1937 (2nd ed. Paris: Perrin, 2002; 3rd ed. Paris: Les Éditions de l'Abordable, 2016).

• *Carnet inédit, 20 novembre 1891-28 octobre 1893,* Pierre de Nolhac, critical edition with introduction and notes by G. Zuccheli. Bologna: Sezione arti grafiche dell'instituto "Aldini-Valeriani," 1969-1970.

• *Ils ont sauvé Versailles, de 1789 à nos jours,* Franck Ferrand. Paris: Perrin, 2003.

• *Pierre de Nolhac,1859-1936,* Claire Salvy. Polignac: Éditions du Roure, 2010.

• *Versailles. Le Palais en 1900,* Maurice Bedon, Collection "Mémoire en images." Saint-Cyr-sur-Loire: A. Sutton Éditions, 2009.

• *Versailles d'antan – Versailles à travers la carte postale ancienne,* André Damien in collaboration with Pierre Garde, Collection "Monique Lehuard et Didier Bertin." Paris: HC éd., 2009 (2nd ed. 2016).

• *Le Versailles des Présidents. 150 ans de de vie républicaine chez le Roi Soleil,* Fabien Oppermann, Collection "Lieux et expressions du pouvoir." Paris: Fayard, Versailles, Palace of Versailles Research Center, 2015.

• *Versailles. Vie artistique, littéraire et mondaine, 1889-1939,* under the direction of Catherine Gendre, in collaboration with the Lambinet Museum. Paris: Somogy Art Editions, 2003.

• *La France du XIXᵉ siècle, 1814-1914,* Francis Démier, Collection "Points Histoire." Paris: éd. Seuil, 2000 (2nd ed. 2014).

• *Mémoires de Boni de Castellane, 1867-1932,* introduction and notes by Emmanuel de Waresquiel, Collection "L'Histoire en mémoires." Paris: Perrin, 2015.

ONLINE SOURCES
• Famille de Nolhac, blog de Martine Hédou (*Nolhac family, Martine Hédou's blog*), nolhac.wordpress.com
• Pierre de Nolhac par Thierry Bajou (*Pierre de Nolhac by Thierry Bajou*), Institut national d'histoire de l'art, inha.fr
• Gallica, Bibliothèque nationale, gallica.bnf.fr